HE DREAMED ABOUT
ANNA CHING...

...When he kissed her, she caught fire, clawing at him while sucking wildly on his tongue. Her skin was incredibly smooth and firm as he kissed and nipped his way down her body. The taste and smell of the girl caused sensations in Tracker that were totally new to him. He had been with many women, and he didn't know if this one was different because she was Chinese, or simply because she *was* different from other women...

The dream had been so real that his physical desire for the dead Chinese girl was frightening.

He would begin his search along the Barbary Coast, and the trail would lead him to the Tong...and to Anna Ching's killer.

TOM CUTTER
TRACKER 6
THE BARBARY COAST TONG

AVON
PUBLISHERS OF BARD, CAMELOT, DISCUS AND FLARE BOOKS

DEDICATION

For Anna & Christopher

AVON BOOKS
A division of
The Hearst Corporation
1790 Broadway
New York, New York 10019

First Avon Printing, May 1985

AVON TRADEMARK REG. U.S. PAT. OFF. AND IN OTHER COUNTRIES, MARCA REGISTRADA, HECHO EN U.S.A.

Printed in the U.S.A.

WFH 10 9 8 7 6 5 4 3 2 1

[Prologue]

Even while he was in bed with the beautiful Chinese girl there on the outskirts of the slum known as Chinatown, Inspector Neil Colby's mind was on the streets and wharves that comprised San Francisco's Barbary Coast. He had been working on a case involving a white slavery ring for months now, and still had not been able to catch a break. He knew who was behind it—the so-called Barbary Coast Tong—but he had been unable to get to the leaders of the tong, leaders who—according to the word on the streets—were Caucasian. He wasn't all that sure he believed this, because he had worked Chinatown long enough to know that the Chinese did not contaminate their tongs with white men. The only other explanation was that it couldn't be a legitimate tong, and yet it employed Chinese hatchet men—

"You are disturbed," the girl's voice said from behind him.

He had been sitting up in bed, smoking a cigar while she slept after their lovemaking. He was angry because the problem on the Coast was keeping him from concentrating fully on her, and she certainly deserved a man's full attention.

He turned to face her and, as always every time he looked at her, fell in love with her all over again.

Her hair was a long, shiny black curtain that she kept sweeping away from her face with a short movement of her head or hand, and it was parted just off center to the left. She was taller and much fuller figured than the average Chinese girl, and incredibly lovely. She was a constant source of torment for Colby because, aside from her, he hated the Chinese.

Yet she was different.

5

"Can you talk about it?" she asked, touching his shoulder.

"No...not to you. I don't want to involve you in matters concerning my job—"

"But I am involved, am I not?" she asked, leaning her head on his shoulder now so that he could smell the fragrant bouquet of her hair and her skin.

"Yes..."

"Is it the Barbary Coast that occupies your mind, or Chinatown?"

"You see right through me."

She kissed his shoulder and said, "I know you well."

He turned to face her, took her in his muscular arms and kissed her, softly at first and then with the intense passion that she always aroused in him, which he feared because it was beyond his ability to control.

"You will not evade my questions so easily," she said after the kiss.

"It's the Coast," he said, "and the white slavers."

"Can I help?"

"No!"

"You are being foolish."

"I do not want you involved."

"Again..." she said, because she had heard those words so many times during the past few months. "I am not a child, Colby, who must be shielded and protected. This is my city, Chinatown is my home—"

"The Coast is not Chinatown," he said, interrupting her.

"It is the same, only the color of the faces is different."

"Not so different," he muttered, and cursed because he knew he had aroused her curiosity now.

"What do you mean?" she asked, and then suddenly she understood. "I have heard of something called the Barbary Coast Tong. Is this what troubles you?

"I don't think it's a legitimate tong," he said, thinking in spite of his fears that she *could* possibly help.

"I can find out," she assured him. "You had only to ask."

"I didn't want to..."

"Lu Hom will help, as well, if I ask him—"

Colby's sharp, bitter laugh cut her off.

"Your brother and I don't see eye to eye, Anna."

"He has worked with a white man before at my request," she reminded him.

"Yes," he said with distaste. "Tracker."

He had heard of Tracker since his arrival in San Francisco a year earlier, but had never met the man. Still, he disliked him because of his previous relationship with Anna Ching, which had also taken place before his arrival.

"Please," she said, because she knew what he was thinking.

"I'm sorry," he said, "it's just that when I think of him...and you..."

"Tracker was a dear friend, Colby, but we have not seen each other for over a year."

"You still have feelings for him, though," Colby said, tormenting himself further.

"I have never denied that, but you are here with me, not him. Does that not mean anything to you?" she asked, running her hand over his hard-muscled chest.

"Yes," he said, taking her by the arms, "it means everything."

"I will help you, Colby. I will find out things for you about this Barbary Coast Tong—"

He silenced her with a kiss, then said, "Later," and pushed her down on the bed.

They did not discuss it again until much later.

At that moment, the leader of the Barbary Coast Tong was addressing two of his underlings, in the basement of a building on California Street. The two listeners were Chinese and resented the fact that they worked for a white man. But his money helped ease their resentment.

"Colby is beginning to be a nuisance," he said. "He must be dealt with."

"As you wish, master," one of the men said.

To the right of their master stood his number one man, a white man called Mannion. This man was feared throughout the tong and on the wharves, for he was a man of tremendous strength who enjoyed inflicting pain almost as much as he enjoyed killing. He did both, often and well, in the service of the master.

"You will obey Mannion as you would me," the master went on, "and if I hear that anyone has not done so, you two shall pay."

"No one will disobey him, master. We will tell the others."

"Go then, and be ready when you are called upon. Tell the others to always be ready."

"Yes, master," the Chinese men said, and bowed their way out of the room.

"I hate these coolies," Mannion said in his gruff voice.

"They're valuable to us," the leader said. "Using them confuses the police."

"Colby," Mannion said, a wealth of hatred contained in that one name.

"Yes, Preston has himself a potential hero there," the leader said, speaking of Chief Preston, the man in charge of the Chinatown district. "We will just have to see that he becomes a dead hero, Mannion. That's your job."

"The pleasure," Mannion said with obvious relish, "will be all mine. If there's anything I hate more than a coolie, it's a lawman."

"I count on that daily, Mannion," the other man said. "Is the latest shipment of girls ready to go?"

"Yes."

"See to it, then, and afterward see to Colby."

"Yes."

After Mannion left the man who had created the Barbary Coast Tong stood up and walked to a bar he had built along the left wall. One thing he had in common with the masters of the legitimate tongs in Chinatown was that he rarely left the confines of his home, which meant that he kept it well stocked with everything he could possibly need. He poured himself a glass of expensive port and then picked up a small bell and rang it.

The small Chinese girl entered through the same door Mannion had used to leave. She was clad only in a flimsy garment which allowed him to see her small, pert breasts and her high, firm buttocks. At seventeen she had already been sold, but before she was delivered he took it upon himself to break her in, so that the customer would be satisfied.

"The bed, Joy," he said, putting down his glass. He removed his jacket and started to unbutton his shirt.

The girl hung her head and walked through the partition in the corner of the room, where she removed her garment and climbed into a large bed. When he was nude he approached the bed and the girl eyed his pulsing erection dully, with no expression. She had learned quickly that to allow her revulsion to show on her face resulted only in pain.

He stood before her, still holding his glass of port, and said smiling, "We have one or two lessons left, my dear, so let us get to them, shall we?"

[1]

When the man walked into the lobby of Farrell House (located just two blocks from San Francisco's fashionable Portsmouth Square) Shana Sullivan was not at her customary position behind the front desk. Not that she'd quit the hotel/gambling house—something the fiery redhead did once or twice a month. This time Shana had asked Deirdre Long to cover for her.

Deirdre was not particularly happy about it because she had a sneaking suspicion she knew where Shana had to go "for a little while."

She would have bet her forty-nine percent of the hotel that Shana was in Tracker's bed. Now, she knew perfectly well that Tracker was not a one-woman man, and that she shared him with Shana on an almost regular basis, but that didn't mean she had to like it. In fact, she hated it, and she hated Tracker for putting her in that position. Her resentment toward Tracker, however, was tempered by her love for him, which was beyond her ability to change.

In any case, Deirdre was behind the desk when the man approached and she put aside her annoyance so she could give him a smile as she asked, "Can I help you, sir?"

"Yes. I was informed that I could find a man called Tracker at this hotel. Is that correct?"

"Do you have business with him?"

"I do, if he is here."

"If you'll have a seat, sir, someone will be out to speak to you shortly."

"Thank you."

The drill was the same, no matter who was handling the desk. Anyone who asked for Tracker had to see Duke first. Although no one knew for certain what

Tracker did to make his money, Deirdre had become privy to at least some of Tracker's secrets because he'd had to rush to her rescue a few months ago when she got herself in a jam in Oklahoma trying to work one of her dead father's scams.* Her father had been Frenchie Longo, King of the Con Men. Then he'd won this hotel, and died trying to turn it into something that would support his daughter legally. She had been roped into trying one last con, however, by an old colleague of her father's, and Tracker had saved her bacon.

She snagged a passing bellboy and told him to find Duke Farrell and send him to the front desk. She hoped that the man would convince Duke to go find Tracker, because it would be her pleasure to send someone up to his room and interrupt him and Shana doing... whatever it was they were doing!

Shana Sullivan was a tall, full-bodied, red-headed ball of fire and her enthusiasm and inventiveness in bed never ceased to amaze Tracker. She was so different from the more inhibited Deirdre. It was probably the huge gap between the two women's personalities that made it impossible for Tracker to prefer one over the other.

Shana was sitting astride Tracker, his huge erection buried to the hilt in her while she rubbed the nipples of her large breasts back and forth over his face. Finally he was able to capture one cherry nipple between his teeth and he proceeded to suck on it while she rode him hard and fast. This wasn't one of her more inventive maneuvers, but it seemed to be a favorite of hers.

Her head was thrown back now and Tracker could feel the rush of completion rising up from him when someone knocked on the door.

"That bitch!" Shana hissed from between her teeth.

"Who, Deirdre?"

"Who else? I asked her to cover for me for a little while, and she probably guessed I was up here with you."

She stopped bouncing on him because she had in-

*Tracker #5: *The Oklahoma Score.*

tended to savor her orgasm and had no intention of rushing it so he could answer the door.

"Answer it now," she said, picking her hips up so he could pop out of her, "and get rid of her."

The air was cool on his shaft, which was slick with her juices. He pulled his pants on to go and answer the door. He disagreed with Shana that it was Deirdre. His money was on Duke, and he was right.

"Interrupting?" Duke asked. He was almost a foot shorter than the six-foot-four Tracker and had to crane his neck to look up at the bigger man.

"Of course," Tracker said. "For something important, I hope."

"A man downstairs wants to see you."

"There's a lady up here with the same idea." Duke easily guessed who the lady was, since he had just spoken to Deirdre. "What's he got to offer?"

"Money?"

"How much?"

"He's wearing a hell of a lot, so who knows?"

Tracker said, "All right, put him in the office and keep him company. I'll be down directly."

"Directly."

"Yeah, that's later than shortly, but sooner than later. Okay?"

"You're the boss."

"Sometimes I wonder."

Tracker closed the door and shed his pants. Shana waited impatiently on the bed, her mass of fiery hair in a tangle, her breasts heaving, nipples still swollen with passion.

She was an incredibly sensuous sight.

"You're not going to rush away, Tracker," she informed him, cupping his balls in one hand and grasping his cock in the other. "Not unless you want to leave without these."

"Well," Tracker said, since he didn't have any intention of rushing, "since you put it that way..."

When Tracker finally appeared in the office Duke rose from behind the desk and said, "Here he is now."

The man turned to look at Tracker as he stood in

12

the doorway and said, "I am not accustomed to being kept waiting, sir."

"Well," Tracker said, "since I don't know who the hell you are I can't say that it worries me."

"I explained that you had other business to attend to—" Duke started, but Tracker cut him off.

"I'm not accustomed to explaining myself to anyone. Duke, you can go."

"Sure," Duke said, although he didn't need to be told. No one sat in on Tracker's business discussions.

After Duke left Tracker walked around behind the desk and sat down. He reached into the bottom drawer and removed a bottle of bourbon.

"Can I offer you a drink, or aren't you accustomed to that, either?"

"I will take a drink, thank you."

Tracker nodded, took out two glasses and poured two fingers into each. He made no move to bring the drink to the man, who looked annoyed at having to get up to get it.

He was about six feet tall, well fed and, as Duke had said, certainly well dressed. He appeared to be in his late fifties, his black hair shot with gray and his bushy mustache entirely gray.

"I was told that you were unorthodox and imperti-nent—"

Tracker didn't bother to ask the man who had told him that. It didn't matter.

"I prefer to think that I do my job my way," he said, interrupting the man. "I'm at a disadvantage here, seeing as how you know who I am."

"Yes, of course," the man said. "To business, then. My name is Tinsdale, Walter J. Tinsdale."

The man paused, Tracker supposed, so that Tracker could express some sort of reaction to the name. When he didn't, the man went on.

"You might have heard of me."

"I have."

Tinsdale's business was thought to be politics, but Tracker knew that the man was not a politician. In-stead, he owned politicians: He backed their campaigns, and from that time on they belonged to him. Tinsdale

13

was what was known as a player—usually a gambler's term, it also applied to the world of politics.

"Yes, well, I've come to you with a very personal problem, Mr. Tracker—"

"Just Tracker is fine."

"Very well...Tracker. My problem is of an extremely personal nature, and involves my daughter, Melody."

"What about her?"

"She's missing."

Tracker poured himself another drink and said, "Go to the police, Mr. Tinsdale."

"You don't understand. I wouldn't know who to trust in the police department."

"That's not an unusual problem, but they're still better equipped to handle this sort of thing."

"No, no," Tinsdale said with increasing annoyance, "you still don't understand. Let me explain."

"All right, explain."

"Thank you. My daughter has disappeared and I'm sure that her disappearance has something to do with the Barbary Coast Tong. Do you know what that is?"

"I've heard talk," Tracker said. The Barbary Coast Tong virtually controlled the drug trade along the Coast and, some said, was moving into Chinatown. Some said the tong also dealt in the white slave market.

"You see then why I cannot go to the police. This tong is bound to be paying them off, and how would I know who to trust?"

"I'm sure you bankroll one or two cops as well as politicians, Mr. Tinsdale," Tracker said frankly.

"I am not on good terms with the police," Tinsdale said, "and I do not think they would put forward their best effort."

"Then hire a private detective or a Pinkerton. There are a lot of agencies in San Francisco now."

"I want to hire you."

"I'm not a private investigator," Tracker said, although he knew he often acted in the same capacity as one.

"I still want you."

"Mr. Tinsdale, my business is the recovery of missing

or stolen property, for which I am paid half of that property's worth. This does not apply to people."

"There's something else, then. Something that I'm sure will interest you."

"What's that?"

"The diamond."

"What diamond?"

"The one I gave Melody last month for her eighteenth birthday. It's set in a ring, and it is worth $25,000."

"Really."

"Yes. I will pay you half that amount if you should recover the diamond or my daughter."

"Let me understand this. You're not proposing a package deal. I don't have to come up with both in order to earn the money? You'll be satisfied with one or the other?"

"Correct."

"If I find the diamond and not your daughter, you'll still pay me?"

"Yes," Tinsdale said patiently.

"I find that proposal a little odd."

"Tracker, I'm banking on the fact that you're a decent man."

"That's a fact?"

Tinsdale ignored the remark and said, "I don't think that if you found the diamond you would abandon the search for my daughter. I'm banking on that, Tracker."

"Well," Tracker said after a moment, "you're a gambler, Tinsdale, I'll give you that."

"You'll take the job?"

"I think you're backing a three-legged horse, but yes, I'll accept the job. Another drink?"

"Yes," Tinsdale said, "I rather think I need one."

Tracker took all the pertinent information from Tinsdale, including a rundown on the men his daughter was seeing. At eighteen—even at seventeen, Tinsdale added—his daughter was rather precocious and, he admitted, experienced when it came to men.

When Tracker asked for his daughter's description Tinsdale produced a tintype of the girl. Tracker saw a lovely girl who had developed physically beyond her

15

years. He could believe that she was experienced in handling men.

"Can I keep this for a while?"

"As long as you like," Tinsdale said, rising. "Tracker, I'll have to ask you to keep all of this quiet. If my enemies ever got a hold of this—"

"I am not a talkative man, Tinsdale."

"No," Tinsdale said, eyeing the big man critically, "I don't suppose you are. I was told, however, that you are a competent man. I hope that's true."

"I get by."

"Yes, well, I'll leave you one of my cards so that you'll know where to get in touch with me."

Tracker stood and took the proffered card but did not immediately read it. Instead he tucked it away in his shirt pocket.

"Well, thank you for accepting the job, Tracker. I'm sure you'll...you'll do your best."

"I'll be in touch, Tinsdale."

Tinsdale looked as if he were waiting for Tracker to see him to the door, but when Tracker made no move to do so the man left without further words.

Tracker sat down and poured himself another drink. He had finished that one and was pouring another when Duke came in.

"Is Shana back on the desk?" Tracker asked him.

"Yes. I had to get between her and Deirdre to avoid a battle."

"Good man."

Duke had spoken to Tracker about the two women before, and it had never done any good, so he kept his thoughts on the subject to himself. He liked Shana well enough, but he was especially fond of Deirdre and didn't want to see her get hurt.

"Working?" Duke asked.

"Yeah."

"When are you leaving?"

"I'm not. I'll be working right here in San Francisco."

"Oh. Well, if you need any help you know where to come."

"Yeah, I do, Duke. Thanks."

Duke wanted to ask what the job was—he always wanted to ask—but he didn't.

"I've, uh, got some paperwork to do," Duke said.

Tracker looked up at him, put the bottle away and stood.

"I'll get out of your way."

Tracker owned the hotel—fifty-one percent, anyway—but he didn't really run it. This he left to Duke. The former con man had taken to hotel management immediately and during the time he'd been in the job the hotel's profits had increased considerably.

"I'm thinking about hiring another cook," Duke said, seating himself behind the desk. "The dinner crowd is starting to become unmanageable."

"Whatever you think is best."

Duke knew the big man trusted him; it was an enormous source of pride to him. He had known Tracker a long time, had fronted for him since Tracker won the hotel, and knew that he trusted very few men.

"I'll be in the saloon for a while if you need me for anything, Duke."

"And after that?"

"After that I'll be working, and I don't know where I'll be."

"Well, remember where *I* am."

Tracker looked at his friend—one of his very few friends—and said, "I'll remember."

[2]

Neil Colby was worried when he left Anna Ching that morning. He shouldn't have agreed to allow her to try and help him. Colby hoped that she'd limit her assistance to asking her brother to help him.

Colby went directly to the Chinatown police station where he learned that Chief Preston wanted to see him as soon as he arrived. He went to the chief's office and knocked.

"Come in."

When he entered the chief was standing behind his desk expectantly.

Chief of Police Ansel Preston was a tall man with silvery hair and a neatly groomed brush mustache. He was in his early fifties and dressed extremely well for a cop. The payoffs from the Chinese gambling halls were generous.

"About time you got here, Colby," he said gruffly.

"I'm a half hour early, sir."

"Hmph! A good policeman should be even earlier than that," Ansel Preston said, and Colby wanted to ask, how would you know?

They were not friends and never would be. Colby considered Preston a puppet for politicians and anybody else who offered to pay him enough, like the Chinese gambling halls. He was sure Preston took payoffs from the tongs, he just didn't know if this included the Barbary Coast Tong.

Preston thought that Neil Colby was the most dangerous kind of cop in the world—an honest one. He had come to San Francisco a year earlier with previous experience in law enforcement, and quickly established himself as an honest, hardworking lawman—just the kind of man Preston didn't need around.

Now Preston was getting pressure from several areas—most notably Chinatown and the Barbary Coast—to put a muzzle on Colby.

"You're making waves, Colby," Preston said without further preamble.

"I thought that was my job."

"It seems to be your specialty," Preston returned.

"Chief—"

"Colby, if I get any more complaints about your harassment techniques I'm gonna put you back in uniform and assign you to roust drunks on California Street."

Well, Colby thought, at least I'd still be near the docks.

"Yes, sir."

Preston was sure Colby's age was part of his problem. About thirty, the man had a lot to learn about police work. Lesson number one should have been that you don't hassle the people with the money, but Preston wasn't ready to voice that lesson. He was not the kind of man given to tossing his own fat in the fire. Right now Colby's youth and honesty were dangerous, but maybe the lad would change. Lord knew, Chinatown had altered enough people—including Ansel Preston.

"Anything else, sir?"

"Yes. I've heard some rumblings about Walter Tinsdale's daughter."

"She's a wild one," Colby said, and Preston frowned and wondered if Colby was speaking from personal experience.

"Well, I've heard that she hasn't been seen for a while and may be missing."

"Did Tinsdale report her missing?"

"No, and he wouldn't, not to me, anyway. I suspect that if she is gone he's hired somebody—maybe even the Pinkertons—to find her."

"What do you want me to do?"

"I want you to find out what's going on. If the girl is missing I want to know if it's her own doing."

Colby wasn't sure why Preston was interested, unless he was just looking to get something on Tinsdale. If the chief could dig up some dirt on Tinsdale, he would certainly be able to use it to launch a political career.

"That's all. Keep me informed."

"Yes, sir."

Initially, Colby had been prepared to resist the assignment, but on second thought it might coincide with his current investigation. The Barbary Coast Tong supposedly dealt in the white slave market as well as the drug trade, and Melody Tinsdale—young, fair-haired and full-bodied—was certainly white slaver material.

Preston might have inadvertently given Neil Colby a new angle. Colby had something to be thankful to the man for—for a change.

Lu Hom did not like his sister's request, and he let her know it.

"You ask too much."

Since Tracker and Lu Hom had broken up the White Pigeon Tong, Anna Ching's brother had worked on his own, making money any way he could. He had not joined another tong but he occasionally worked for them, usually as an enforcer.

"Do you know of such a tong?" his sister asked.

"I do."

"Then you can help—"

"I helped one of your white lovers once before," he interrupted. "Now you have another."

"I do not ask your approval of my lovers—"

"That is obvious."

"—as you do not ask such approval from me."

"I do not take *lo fan* lovers."

"I do not wish to argue this with you. You are my brother, I am asking for your help. If you refuse, I will help Colby myself."

"Help him, then," Lu Hom said. "He is your lover."

Anna Ching stood up, said, "I will," and promptly left Lu Hom's room on Dupont Street.

Lu Hom had no way of knowing that was the last time he would ever see his sister.

Tracker's experiences with Chinatown had been limited since he had seen Anna Ching the year before. He had thought of the beautiful girl often, but had never made an effort to get in touch with her. Their two worlds were totally different and neither fit easily into the other's.

20

This thought was brought home to Tracker as he walked through the Chinatown streets head and shoulders taller than everyone else. Not that white faces were rare in this part of Chinatown with its gambling dens, but it *was* rare for the Chinese people to see a *lo fan* of Tracker's stature and bearing.

Tracker had gone to Chinatown first rather than the Barbary Coast because he wanted to check up on the Barbary Coast Tong. He'd questioned Duke because his friend always seemed to have his finger on the pulse of San Francisco, but all Duke could tell him was that it was rumored not to be controlled by the Chinese. Still, if he was going to get information about a tong, he would get it in Chinatown.

And if he happened to run across Anna Ching in the process, that wouldn't be so bad either.

Actually, Tracker was walking along Dupont Street, Ross Alley, Sacramento Street and some others where the *lo fan* went to gamble hoping to spot Anna or her brother Lu Hom.

Tracker didn't know what had happened to Lu Hom after he and the deadly little Chinaman had destroyed the White Pigeon Tong. He wasn't even sure Lu Hom would speak to him if they met, but it was a long shot and the big man was a long shot player from way back.

When Tracker turned into Dupont Street he became aware of some commotion ahead. Disturbances were not unheard of in Chinatown; they were usually caused by a dispute over gambling or a girl. Tracker had only bedded one Chinese girl—Anna Ching—but he supposed that Chinese whores held a certain fascination for some Caucasians.

He moved toward the crowd and decided to stay on the outskirts of it when he saw the two cops. They were in the center of the circle of people, one of them attempting to hold back the crowd while the other bent over a still form.

The police were too intent on other matters to notice Tracker towering over everybody. However, his height gave him the advantage of an unobscured view and he could see that the person on the ground was a woman. But the cop who was holding back the crowd blocked his view of the woman's face.

21

"She's dead, all right," one of the policemen said.

"Come on, get back," the other told the crowd, and moved slightly.

Tracker felt a shock ripple down to his toes when he saw the woman's face.

It was Anna Ching.

Even as he walked back to the hotel in a state of shock—you don't realize how much you liked somebody until you see them dead—Tracker knew that he'd be getting a visit from the police. Chief Preston would certainly remember his relationship with the dead girl and wouldn't pass up this opportunity to question him.

When he entered the hotel Shana was on the desk, and she knew from his solemn expression that something was wrong.

"Tracker—"

"Where's Duke?"

"In the office. What's—"

He marched past the desk without giving her a chance to say anything further. She watched his back until he disappeared into the office.

Duke looked up from the desk as Tracker entered, and frowned at the expression on the big man's face.

"What the hell happened to you?"

"Remember a Chinese girl I knew about a year ago? Anna Ching?"

"That time you and Will Sullivan went to Chinatown?"

"Right."

"I remember."

"She's dead."

"What?"

"I just came from Chinatown where she was found on the street. She'd been stabbed."

"Does this have something to do with Tinsdale—"

"I was working, that's why I went to Chinatown, but I don't think it's connected. Anyway, I think I can expect a visit from Chief Preston—"

"Why? Just because you knew the girl a year ago?"

"The lawman mentality," Tracker said. "He'll be here and if he finds out I was in Chinatown he'll try to make

22

me his guest for a while. If that happens, I won't be free to—"

"To find out who killed her," Duke said, because he knew that was what Tracker had on his mind. The girl was a friend of his, maybe more, and somebody had killed her. Tracker would not be able to let that go without doing something.

"When he gets here I'll be in my room," Tracker said. "With cover?"

"Yes," Tracker said, thoughtfully. "Deirdre."

Duke would have thought that Tracker would use Shana as his cover, but perhaps he trusted Deirdre more.

"Will she go along with it?"

"No question," Tracker said, thinking of how he and Deirdre had worked together on the Oklahoma thing—and of how she felt about him. "No question at all."

Deirdre was agreeable, but she also wanted some answers if she was going to lie to the police.

"Do I get to know what this is about?" she asked when they were in Tracker's room.

"You get to ask."

"But I don't get any answers?"

"Not right now, Deirdre. I'm not sure myself yet what's going on, so I don't know how much is safe to tell you." She was about to protest when he said, "You trust me, don't you?"

She stopped short at that question and then said in an exasperated tone, "You know I do, but dammit, sometimes you infuriate me!"

He grinned at the beautiful blonde and said, "That's part of my charm, isn't it?"

"When is this cop supposed to be here?"

"I'm not sure. It could be a while."

She regarded him for a few moments with her hands on her hips, then reached behind her to undo her dress.

"Well," she said, letting the dress fall to the floor around her ankles, "we might as well get comfortable."

[3]

They were still getting comfortable when the expected knock came at the door. From the weight behind the knocking fist, they knew it had to be the police.

"Let me get dressed," Deirdre said, struggling to get out from under Tracker.

"No," he said, taking his weight off her and standing up. "Stay like that. It'll add to the story."

She stared at him for a moment, then grabbed for the sheet and pulled it up around her neck with a defiant look.

"Okay," he said, grinning. "Okay."

Tracker considered answering the door naked, but decided to pull on his pants first.

It was Chief Ansel Preston, as well dressed as Tracker remembered, with two uniformed policemen behind him.

"Hello, Tracker."

"Preston," Tracker said, feigning surprise. "What can I do for you?"

"Just a little conversation, that's all," the policeman said. "Mind if I come in?"

"Uh, well, actually, Preston, this isn't a good time for a visit."

"Is that so?" the lawman asked. He peered past Tracker and then frowned at what he saw. He realized his men were also looking into the room and told them, "You two wait down the hall."

They exchanged glances and with a last brief gaze past Tracker, moved off down the hall, as ordered.

"How long has she been here?" Preston then asked Tracker.

"Quite a while, I think," Tracker said. "I'm not sure. We came up after lunch—"

"You've been up here with the lady all this time?"

24

"Preston," Tracker said in a tone meant to imply that they were both men of the world.

"Do you mind if I ask the lady myself?"

"I don't mind if she doesn't," Tracker said. He turned and said to Deirdre, "Chief Preston is here, Dee. He'd like to ask you a couple of questions. Is that all right?"

"Is he a gentleman?" she asked loud enough for Preston hear.

Tracker turned to look at Preston, who stared back stolidly.

"I think so."

"All right, then."

Tracker gestured to the lawman and said, "Preston?"

Preston preceded Tracker into the room; the big man closed the door behind them.

"Excuse me, Miss...Long, isn't it?" he asked, frowning. "You own the hotel, isn't that right?"

"You have an excellent memory, chief," she said, smiling dazzlingly. Tracker could see that Deirdre was actually enjoying her performance. She even allowed the bedsheet to slip down a bit, showing some cleavage which Preston would have to have been blind to miss...and not appreciate.

"Uh, yes," Preston said, appearing uncomfortable. "Miss Long, when did you and, uh, Mr. Tracker come up here to his room?"

"I think it was right after lunch, wasn't it?" she said, looking at Tracker.

"That's what I said."

"And you have been up here together all this time?"

"That's right."

"Together?"

"I would have noticed if I was alone, Chief Preston."

"Yes, of course."

"Do you mind telling us what this is all about?" she asked, using the opportunity to find out what Tracker had not told her.

Preston turned to Tracker and said in an official-sounding voice, "You had a relationship with an Oriental girl named Anna Ching about a year back, didn't you?"

"I knew her, yeah," Tracker said. "That's just about the time we first met, too, isn't it?"

Preston ignored the question.

"Have you seen her since then?"

"No."

"Not at all?"

"No. I don't go to Chinatown much."

"Were you there today, at all?"

"No."

"It wouldn't be hard for me to find a witness to the contrary, you know. Man your size would tend to stand out anywhere, let alone in Chinatown."

"With all due respect, chief, if you had a witness, we wouldn't be talking here, but in your office."

That was true and Preston couldn't deny it.

"Well," he said, rotating his bowler in his hands, "she was found dead today in Chinatown, on Dupont Street."

Both men heard Deirdre's sharp intake of breath.

"How?" Tracker asked.

"She was murdered—stabbed."

"And you thought that I—"

"I'm simply questioning anyone who knew her," Preston interrupted. "I'm not accusing you."

"Well, that's nice."

Preston turned to Deirdre and said, "I'm sorry to have disturbed you, Miss Long."

"That's all right," Deirdre said. She was obviously still shaken by the news.

"Good evening," Preston said, and walked to the door with Tracker. When he stepped out into the hall he turned and said, "If I find out that you've lied to me—"

"Why would I do that, Preston?"

"Our paths haven't crossed in the past year, but that doesn't mean that I haven't kept an eye on you."

Tracker shrugged and said, "There hasn't been all that much to see."

"Maybe not," Preston said, "but I've heard stories about a man who would do just about anything for the right amount of money—"

"If I meet such a man," Tracker told the lawman, "I'll be sure to tell him."

"You do that. You tell him that I'll be watching him even closer from now on."

"Goodnight, chief."

Preston walked down the hall, collected his men and left without further word. Tracker closed the door and turned to face Deirdre, who was getting dressed.

"You knew."

"I knew."

"And I'm your alibi?"

"Yes."

"Do you know anything about it?"

He shook his head.

"I was there when they found her, that's all. I was in Chinatown on another matter."

"Tracker—" she said, shaking her head.

"I'm sorry, Dee.".

"I'm sorry, too," she said, fully dressed now. "I'm sorry your...friend is dead, and I'm sorry you didn't trust me enough to tell me. I remember her, you know."

"I didn't want to tell you more than you needed to know. Didn't hurt that you were so surprised, either."

"I suppose so. I just wish you trusted me as much as I trust you."

"If I didn't trust you, Dee," he said, "I wouldn't have asked you to come up here."

"Why did you?" she asked, frowning curiously. "Why did you ask me and not...Shana?"

He told her something then that he didn't ever think he would.

"I guess I feel a little closer to you than I do to Shana, Dee." Her expression softened until he added, "After all, we are partners."

Then her face clouded and she snapped, "Damn you!"

"What's the matter?" he asked as she strode toward the door.

"You would have to ruin it, wouldn't you."

She stormed out of the room. Tracker started to dress, swearing that he never had understood women, and never would.

"How'd it go with Preston?" Duke asked when Tracker came down to the lobby. "He didn't look too happy when he left."

"I guess that was because he had to leave without me. Did he leave anybody across the street?"

27

"Nobody in uniform. Might take him some time to send a plainclothes man down here."

"He will, though."

"What are you going to do? About the Chinese girl, I mean?"

"I've got a job."

"Sure, Tracker."

Tracker frowned at Duke and said, "I'm getting paid to do a job, Duke. I don't have time—"

"Well, if you happen to make time, let me know."

"I'll be in the saloon. There ain't much I can do to-night."

"I guess not."

The silence between the two friends was awkward. Finally Tracker broke away and walked toward the dining room. Duke figured that even if Tracker was going to go after the girl's killer he wouldn't want to get anyone else involved. He also knew that there wasn't much sense in arguing about it. If the big man got into trouble and needed help, he'd hear about it soon enough.

[4]

Tracker had been in the saloon only half an hour, sitting morosely in a corner with a bottle of whiskey, when Duke came in looking for him.

"How long has he been like that?" Duke asked Will Sullivan.

"Since he came in. Must be something eating at him."

"Yeah. Friend of his got killed today. A girl."

"Who?"

"Chinese girl named Anna Ching. Remember her from a year ago?"

"Sure. That time he had me take him to Chinatown. Cured me of gambling there, too."

"Oh yeah? Where do you do it now?" Duke asked. Will gave him a hard stare and the smaller man walked over to where Tracker was sitting.

"Tracker?"

"Yeah."

Duke figured that the bottle must have been full when Tracker started. It was only half full now. Still, he knew Tracker's capacity for liquor, and the big man wasn't anywhere near being drunk.

"There's a policeman here asking to talk to you."

"Preston?" Tracker asked, looking up at Duke.

"No, says his name is Colby, Inspector Colby."

"Preston send him?"

"He says not. He says he's here on his own, and not as a cop."

"What's on his mind?"

"He wouldn't say, just that he wants to talk to you."

Tracker thought a moment, then said, "All right."

"Should I put him in the office?"

"No, bring him in here. I'll talk to him here."

29

Duke hesitated a moment. "All right."

He came back a few moments later with a tall, well-built, clean-shaven man in his early thirties.

"Tracker, Inspector Colby," Duke said, making introductions.

"Sit down, Inspector. Have a drink," Tracker said.

Colby sat down stiffly, then looked pointedly at Duke.

"Thanks, Duke."

"Sure," Duke said to Tracker. "I've got work to do."

Tracker waved at Will to bring another glass. He filled it and pushed it over to the inspector.

"What's this about?" he asked. "My friend says that Chief Preston didn't send you."

"That's right, he didn't," the man said, ignoring the glass in front of him.

"What can I do for you, then?"

"I want to know when you last saw Anna Ching."

"I thought you said Preston didn't send you?"

Colby made a face which Tracker construed as his opinion of his superior and said, "He didn't."

"Then what's your connection?"

"It's personal."

"Personal," Tracker repeated. "You mean—" and he stopped, because he knew what Colby meant. "I see."

"I don't care if you see or not," Colby said forcefully. "I want to know when you saw Anna last."

Tracker stared at the other man, who was just a few years younger than himself, and decided that he would give him the benefit of an answer. If he didn't, the conversation would probably go no further without some violence. It might have been interesting, since the Inspector looked as if he could handle himself in a fight, but it wasn't necessary—yet.

"All right, Inspector," Tracker said. "I don't like your tone, but I'm going to give you your answer. I haven't seen Anna Ching for over a year—until today, when I saw her dead."

"You told Preston you weren't anywhere near Chinatown," Colby said, his tone accusing.

"And I lied—but you're not here officially, Colby, so I don't expect you to go back to him and tell him that."

"I wouldn't tell Preston if his pants were on fire."

"Well, it looks as if we share an opinion of the good Chief Preston, if nothing else."

"I can't believe that you and Anna haven't seen each other in that long."

"Why not?"

"Because...because you were on her mind—"

"Are you a mind reader?"

Colby shook his head and said, "A man knows when a woman is thinking about another man."

"That sounds too confusing to repeat. Are you going to waste that drink?"

Colby looked at the drink in front of him for a second, then picked it up and downed it.

"Another one?"

"Yeah."

Tracker refilled the glass.

"Shall we start this conversation again from the beginning?" Tracker asked.

"I thought—I thought maybe you'd seen her—" Colby stammered, his anger at Tracker gone. He realized now that he had been hoping that Tracker *had* seen her recently. "I thought you'd know something—"

"No, I don't," Tracker said. "Not yet."

Colby looked down at the second drink as if he had just noticed it, and then drank it. Tracker wasn't sure he should give the man a third.

"I'm going to find out who killed her, Tracker."

"Colby, settle down a minute," Tracker said. He didn't want the man to go off on a drinking binge or a crying jag. Not until he had a chance to see what the man knew, without knowing it.

"What were you working on?" Tracker asked the Inspector.

It was obvious that the man did very little drinking, because two drinks seemed to have had an adverse effect on him already.

"Come on, Colby. Was she helping you with something or did she get killed because some guy thought she was a Chinese whore who didn't want to—"

"Shut up!" Colby shouted, staring murderously at Tracker across the table.

The other customers in the saloon looked over at the two men and saw one man half out of his chair, body

31

shaking with rage while the second man was sitting comfortably, calmly regarding the other.

"Sit down, Colby," Tracker said coldly. "Maybe you're not here officially, but let's see you act like a pro, anyway."

The odds were even for a while as to whether Colby would sit or take a swing at Tracker, but in the end the man sat down.

"She must have been helping you, or you wouldn't have blown up like that. Tell me about it."

"She was just supposed to ask some questions for me," Colby said with a look of anguish. He was being eaten up by guilt over Anna's death. "She was supposed to talk to her brother—"

"Lu Hom? Have you met Lu Hom?"

"Yes."

"Then you know the last thing he'd want to do is help a Caucasian lawman in Chinatown."

"It wasn't Chinatown I was interested in, exactly," Colby explained. "It was the Barbary Coast and something called the Barbary Coast Tong."

"What?"

"The Barbary Coast Tong," Colby said again, frowning at Tracker's reaction to the name. "Does that name mean something to you?"

"Yes, it does."

"What?"

Tracker stared at Colby, who now seemed to be all business. The man's mood changes were too mercurial and too swift for his liking.

"I've just started looking into the Tong myself."

"Why?"

Tracker caught Colby's eyes and held them as he said, "That's personal."

"Look, Tracker, if you know something that could lead to Anna's killer you'd better—"

"I don't know anything, Colby, but I will."

"Why? If you hadn't seen her for a year why should you care?"

"Because we were friends," Tracker replied, simply, "and I don't have that many friends that I can take the loss of one lightly. I think you've worn out your welcome

32

here, Colby—that is, unless you want to make this an official visit."

Colby stared at Tracker for a few moments, then shook his head and said, "No, that won't be necessary." The Inspector stood up, slightly unsteady, and said, "I'm not going to tell Preston about this conversation, Tracker, but don't get in my way on this. I'm going to have Anna's killer."

Sure, Tracker thought, watching Colby's retreating back as he negotiated the distance to the exit, but you'll have to do some growing up first.

Colby was outside his rooming house when they jumped him. There were two of them, and if he hadn't had those two drinks, he might have heard them right away. As it was, they almost had him, which sobered him up real quick.

Their error was in trying to take him quietly, with knives. If they had used guns, he'd have been a dead man. They came at him from opposite sides and since Colby lived in a rooming house on a small, unlit street, the battle went unnoticed.

He was jarred into sobriety by the sharp blade of a knife slicing through the flesh of his left side. Only Colby's excellent reflexes saved him from more serious damage. He executed a somewhat shaky but effective pirouette, which gave him the room he needed to throw a vicious kick, utilizing his knowledge of French kickboxing known as *savate*. He had learned it while living in New Orleans. The kick landed alongside the head of one of the blade men, snapping his neck and killing him instantly. It was an extension of Colby's reflex action, done purely by instinct with no thought involved.

He turned to face the second man, who was just a silhouette in the dark. The man's arms were held out from his sides, and Colby knew that he had a knife in one of his hands. He lay back, waiting for the other man to make the first move. Finally, the man lunged forward with his knife. Colby stepped back in an apparent retreat, shifting his weight to his back leg, and then flicked the front foot out in a powerful front kick which effectively disarmed his attacker. The man, unarmed now, seemed hesitant about what to do, and finally decided that he and his friend had bitten off more than they could chew. He did the only thing he could think of. He ran.

[5]

What Tracker's next move should be was open for debate, and he debated it with himself after returning to his room. He could go to the Barbary Coast, or he could go looking for Lu Hom.

To look for Lu Hom would be futile. He had known that all along, even though he had been doing just that when he went to Chinatown. Of course, he would have settled for finding Anna Ching, but not the way he had ultimately found her. And if trying to help Colby had gotten her killed, might the same thing have happened if Tracker had asked her first? Would he be feeling the guilt that Colby was obviously feeling, as well as the sorrow he was feeling now?

Further questions came to mind, enough to give anyone a headache. *Had* Anna Ching been killed because she was asking questions about the Barbary Coast Tong? And if so, did that mean that by working on one matter, Tracker would also be working on the other? Should he hit the Barbary Coast and take up the trail of Melody Tinsdale, assuming that it would eventually lead to Anna Ching's killer?

He was struggling with these questions—and more—when there was a knock at his door, and he wondered if it was Colby, liquored up further and coming back to take that swing at him. He almost hoped that it was.

It wasn't.

It was Shana.

"Hi," she said.

"Shana."

"Can I come in?"

"Sure."

He backed away to let her in, and then closed the door.

"I heard about...your friend's...death," Shana said, haltingly.

Duke must have told her. He doubted that Deirdre would have.

"I thought maybe I could...help."

"Oh? How?"

"Well, sometimes it helps to be with someone at a time like this," Shana said, moving closer to him.

"Shana," he said, taking her by the shoulders, "we don't need an excuse to be together. If you want to stay here with me, that's fine, but it will be because we want it that way, not because I need a shoulder to cry on. I don't."

"But, I thought you were...close..."

"We were close at one time," Tracker said, "but we were never in love, if that's what you're worried about, Shana."

It was. He could tell by the look of relief that flooded her face.

"Well, I don't have to be on the desk for another half hour," she said, her fingers toying with the buttons on the front of her shirt.

"If that's the case," Tracker said, reaching for the buttons of his own shirt, "you'd better work those buttons a lot faster, woman!"

Their clothes came off quickly, flying in all directions, and when they were naked Tracker pushed her down onto the bed and then stared at her. Her breasts were large and slightly flattened out due to the fact that she was lying down. Her large cherry nipples were already distended in anticipation of his hands and mouth. Shana knew that Tracker loved her breasts, because he always spent so much time sucking on them and fondling them, and she loved it even more than he did.

Her hair was fanned out on the pillow around her head, and he had told her on more than one occasion that if she ever cut her long hair he'd flog her. The tangled mass of hair between her legs testified to the fact that she was a true redhead, and her pubic patch was almost as wild and untamed as the hair on her head. Her eyes were large and green, and they flashed when she was angry or sexually aroused.

He enjoyed studying her, the way she bent her fine long legs, rubbing the heel of her right foot against her left calf, the flatness of her belly, but even more than looking at her he loved to touch her, so finally he joined her on the bed. His mouth sought the nipples of her big, firm breasts as her hands reached for the massive, swollen column of flesh between his legs. She grasped him with both hands and pulled him toward her hot, wet portal, but he wasn't ready for that yet.

He sucked and nipped at her breasts and nipples until she was writhing on the bed beneath him, and suddenly she was coming. It had almost happened several times in the past, but this was the first time Tracker had been able to bring her off simply by sucking her breasts. She pulled at his swollen cock impatiently, but he still wasn't ready. Instead, he moved down so that he could bury his face in the wiry tangle of pubic hair, searching with his tongue. She was wet and ready and he slurped at her juices and then plunged his tongue deep inside of her, flicking it in and out like a miniature cock. Again her body was racked with spasms of pleasure as he brought her off again, and her hands clutched convulsively at the back of his head. He slid his tongue along her slit and concentrated his attention on her incredibly swollen clit. He lashed at it repeatedly and this time she cried out as she came, no longer able to hold it in.

"Oh God, Tracker, put it in me, please! I want you in me! God, how I want you..." she cried out desperately.

In truth he wanted it as badly as she did now, so he plunged into her powerfully, stabbing to her core and bringing a stifled scream of pure delight to her lips.

"Oh God, yes, Tracker..." she moaned as he humped her with long, powerful strokes. Her arms and legs wrapped themselves around him, clasping him tightly to her, their sweat-soaked bodies making sucking noises against each other.

He pressed his mouth over hers, and she opened it and mashed her tongue against his. She kissed and kissed until they were almost drooling on each other, and he reached beneath her to cup her buttocks as he felt the rush of his release building up in his legs. It always seemed to come from his legs, as if he were emptying out from the ankles up, and he knew this one was going to be a beauty!

When they exploded they did so as one and Tracker could have sworn later, looking back, that their dual climax shook the entire hotel—or at least the floor that his room was on. His ejaculation was so powerful that she screamed into his mouth, and the last few spurts as he emptied into her were painful.

"God," she said breathlessly, a few moments later, "it was like...like an explosion, like you had a stick of dynamite in me."

"I may have been the dynamite, honey," he said, licking sweat from the slopes of her breasts, "but you were the fuse."

When Shana dressed and left him lying in bed, kissing him fleetingly, he felt pleasantly fatigued and knew he'd be asleep in seconds. The fiery Shana Sullivan had been just what he needed to put off his decisions until the next morning...

[6]

...But morning did come, and the decisions had to be made.

He had dreamed about Anna Ching, about the first time they had gone to bed together.

When he kissed her, she caught fire, clawing at him while sucking wildly on his tongue. The taste and smell of the girl caused sensations in Tracker that were totally new to him. He had been with many women, and he didn't know if this one was different because she was Chinese, or simply because she was different from other women. Whatever, his hands worked quickly at her clothing, just as her hands worked to undress him.

Her breasts were full and round, with dark brown nipples swollen to an almost incredible size. He pushed her back so that she fell onto the bed, and he tumbled to the mattress with her, careful not to let his entire weight fall on her.

First his mouth sought out her breasts and nipples, sucking and nibbling at them while she writhed beneath him, muttering in Chinese.

Her skin was incredibly smooth and firm as he kissed and nipped his way down her body, pausing to lave her navel with his tongue, and then going on until his nose was nestled in her fragrant nest and his tongue was avidly seeking the taste of her juices.

His first taste of her made him eager, almost desperate for more. He began to run his tongue deep inside of her while she gripped the back of his head and drove her hips up in response to his probings. Her Chinese mutterings had risen in pitch and volume until, as he found her clit and worked her toward a massive orgasm, she was babbling aloud.

As her belly began to tremble he used his hands to pin her thighs to the bed, and then she stiffened as her orgasm seized her. Unable to move her hips she began to drum her fists on the bed and toss her head from side to side. Even in her frenzy she must have realized that by holding her down that way Tracker was somehow increasing the intensity of her climax.

When Tracker felt her tremblings begin to decrease he released her thighs and moved up so that his massive, raging erection was poking at the slippery, slick portal between her legs. She spread her thighs eagerly for him and gasped as he drove the full length of his shaft into her.

She began to mix her Chinese with a smattering of English, although the only words he was able to make out were "Oh, yes," and "please, please..."

Her frenzied movements had caused the curtain of her long black hair to fall across her face like a veil; Tracker used one hand to smooth it away so he could see her better. Some strands were matted to her sweaty forehead, but he plucked them away gently until his view of her lovely face was unobscured. The expression on her face was one of pure lust. As much as he was giving her, she wanted more, and gripped his buttocks in an attempt to get it. As her small hands closed over his buttocks, his massive hands slid beneath her to do the same and from that point on if they had gotten any closer they would have been one person.

As he continued to drive into her he realized that the sounds she was making were not words of any language, now. She was simply moaning or crying out as he drove into her again and again, and as he felt her reaching her climax he increased his pace so that he went with her.

The period afterward was somewhat awkward because neither of them seemed to know what to say. They had both been caught by surprise not only by the intensity of their coupling, but also by the swiftness of the decision to do so.

"I did not anticipate this," she finally said.

"Neither did I," he said.

* * *

40

Tracker awoke with a raging hard-on and lay still for several moments waiting for it to subside. The dream had been so real that his physical desire for the dead Chinese girl was frightening.

When his penis had finally relaxed somewhat he rose from the bed. He walked to the pitcher and basin on his dresser, poured some lukewarm water from one into the other and splashed it onto his face and chest. While he dried himself he realized that his decision had been made. He would continue—or begin—his search for Melody Tinsdale along the Barbary Coast, and the trail would lead him to the Tong and, finally, to Anna Ching's killer.

[7]

Tracker briefly considered using some kind of cover when he started hitting the saloons and gambling houses of the Barbary Coast, but decided against it. If word got around that he was looking for the Tinsdale girl, maybe the Barbary Coast Tong would make an attempt to pay him off, or to kill him. Either way, if he was alert he would be able to turn the move to his advantage. He decided to simply move from place to place, showing the girl's tintype and asking if anyone had seen her.

At breakfast he briefly outlined his plan for Duke, who listened eagerly, but could not contain his curiosity about something.

"Let me ask you something," he said when Tracker had finished.

"What?"

"You don't usually confide in anyone when you're working, not even me. Why now?"

"That's not strictly true, Duke," Tracker said, correcting the smaller man. "Anytime my work keeps me in San Francisco, I take you into my confidence to some degree."

"I guess that's true enough."

"Anyway, I'm not going after one man this time. The Barbary Coast Tong—if it exists—will have a lot of men working for it, and I'm going to end up coming up against one or more of them. I just want you to be aware of what I'm into, in case something happens."

"Well, are you going to prowl the Coast without some kind of backup?"

"No. I plan to ask Will to tag along behind me."

Duke's disappointment at not being asked himself was evident, but he recognized that if it came down to some kind of physical confrontation, Will Sullivan would be of a lot more use than Duke. His forte was conning people, not fighting them.

"If I need your special talents, Duke," Tracker said, as if reading his friend's mind, "I'll put out a call for you, don't worry."

That seemed to satisfy the former con man, and he attacked the remainder of his breakfast in a better frame of mind.

After breakfast Tracker went into the saloon. It wasn't open yet, but he found Will putting the place in order after the previous night's business.

"Thought I'd find you here."

"Stock's got to be checked, and I had to put out a couple of new tables," the former boxer explained. "A couple of fellers got all likkered up and before you knew it, they was at each other with a couple of table legs. Unfortunately, they both ripped them off of different tables."

"Get paid for the damages?"

"Oh yeah. The cops came in and we settled for a payoff all around." Will Sullivan gave Tracker a knowing look, but Tracker had not missed Will's meaning. Instead of making arrests, the police had made the two men pay for the damages, and then had fined them a little extra for themselves before sending them on their way.

"Think you can get someone to cover the bar for you?"

"For how long?"

Tracker shrugged.

"However long I need you for."

"You need somebody to hold your hand in Chinatown again?"

Tracker shook his head.

"The Barbary Coast."

Will Sullivan raised his eyebrows and whistled soundlessly.

"They grow them a little bigger there, and maybe a little meaner, too."

"That's why I need you—to watch my back while I ask some questions."

"They don't take kindly to questions in that part of town."

"I know."

Will shrugged his heavily muscled shoulders and said, "Sure, I can grab somebody and stick them behind the bar. When do you want to go?"

"Just be ready and I'll come and get you."

"Sure."

"Thanks, Will."

"Hey, my little sister would never forgive me if I let anything happen to you. I'd never hear the end of it."

"I appreciate it anyway, Will."

"Sure, Tracker."

Will watched as Tracker walked through the doorway that led from the saloon to the hotel dining room. He'd never seen Tracker in this particular mood before. The death of that Chinese gal must have hit him real hard. He made a mental note to stay extra close on Tracker's heels while they were on the Barbary Coast.

Tracker had one more thing to do before he devoted himself fully to locating the Barbary Coast Tong and Melody Tinsdale.

He had to talk to Deirdre.

Shana was on the desk, but he never even considered asking her where the blonde girl was. Shana was very understanding about Tracker's relationship with Deirdre—more than Deirdre was about his relationship with the fiery redhead—but that didn't mean that Shana never got jealous. She was, after all, still a woman.

Instead, he went to the office where he found Duke and asked him if he knew where Deirdre was.

"I think she said she was going shopping, but she was stopping at her room first. Might still catch her there."

"Thanks."

"You going to work?"

"After I talk to her."

"What about Will?"

"He's going to get someone to take care of the saloon."

"I'll keep my eye on it."

"Thanks."

He left the office and went upstairs to Deirdre's room. When he knocked she answered the door, dressed to go out.

44

"Tracker."

"I wanted to talk to you for a minute, Dee."

"Sure."

She backed away and he stepped into the room and shut the door.

"I wanted you to know that I might not be around so much for the next few days. I'll be working."

"Here in San Francisco."

"That's right."

"On the murder of...of your friend?"

"No," he said, "not exactly, but the thing I'm working on might lead me in that direction."

"I see. Is that all?"

"Yeah, I guess so."

He started to turn and reach for the door but she stopped him by calling his name.

"Tracker."

"Yes?"

"I'm...sorry about your friend's death. I shouldn't have blown up at you the way I did."

"That's okay, Dee. You've got a pretty quick temper, you know."

Her mouth stiffened for a moment, but she caught herself and said, "Yes, I know. I got that from my father."

"Well, there's one thing I'm sure glad you didn't get from Big Frenchie."

She frowned and asked, "What's that?"

"Your looks." He leaned over and kissed her on the cheek. "I'll be seeing you."

"Yes," she said, and he was already through the door and gone when she added, "Be careful."

Mannion was sweating.

Some hours earlier one of the men he had sent to kill Inspector Colby had returned, carrying the body of the second man. The man's excuse was that Colby was a devil, and had moved faster than any man he had ever seen. Such a man could not be killed by just two men, the survivor had said, and Mannion had knocked him down, breaking his jaw in the process. While the man tried to plead with his mouth bleeding, Mannion had hauled him to his feet and effortlessly broken the

45

man's neck. After that he sent for two more men to dispose of the body.

He was sweating because now he had to explain the incident to the leader, who had been known to go into a rage over failure.

Mannion was not especially intelligent, but he was smart enough to realize one thing. He knew that if he hoped to get anywhere in life and not have to work himself to death for monthly wages that would barely support him, he had to obey the leader. The reason he feared the smaller, older, weaker man was because the man was—in Mannion's eyes—a genius, and if Mannion failed to serve him properly, he'd be out on the streets, or dead. With the leader, he stood to be a fairly rich man.

Now he had to convince the leader that the failure was not his fault and, if he was given a second chance, he'd have to make it count.

He'd have to make sure that Inspector Neil Colby was dead before the week was out.

He wiped the perspiration from his face and forehead with his sleeve, took a deep breath, and knocked on the leader's door. It was Colby's fault that he was in this position, and the man would pay dearly.

[8]

California Street was the hub of the Barbary Coast. The largest of the gambling halls lined this street, and shills from each establishment stood out front, extolling the virtues of the particular hall they worked for.

Also working the streets were the Barbary Coast prostitutes, garishly painted ladies who flaunted their nearly bare breasts in an effort to entice passing men to spend some time—and money—on them.

Tracker started at one end of California Street and ran the gamut of prostitutes as he worked the gambling halls, pretending to be taken in by the shills who promised untold delights within.

He started as soon as it got dark, entering a particular hall, doing a little gambling, a little drinking and a little talking. In each place he'd find a receptive ear and start talking about this girl he was looking for. He told a story of how he and the girl were real serious about each other until she decided to take off with his poke one day. She had always talked about going to San Francisco, and his poke had given her enough money to do it.

"Prettiest little thing you'd ever want to see," he said at one point. He was in a place called Crystal's Palace, the fourth such place he had entered so far. He was talking to the bartender in Crystal's.

"They're the ones you gotta watch out for," the bartender said. "The innocent-looking ones."

"Sweet and innocent, she was. Her name was Melody."

"Typical," the barkeep said, shaking his head. "What'd she look like?" The heavy-set man was in his forties. He had thick facial features except for his small, deeply set eyes. Right now those eyes looked hungry, the way they probably always looked when he was talking about women. Tracker suspected that all the man ever got to do when it came to women was talk about them.

"Young, not even nineteen yet, and blonde," Tracker said, trying to sound mournful. "I should have known she was too good to be true."

"Ain't that always the way."

"You know, I've got a tintype of her. Had it made up in New Orleans."

"Yeah?" the man asked, his eyes becoming hungrier. "Let's see it."

"I got it right here," Tracker said, taking it out of his shirt pocket. He affected a sheepish grin and said, "I thought it might come in handy, you know?"

"Sure," the bartender said with great understanding. "You seen the ones they're selling now of the women who ain't wearing nothing?"

"Well," Tracker said regretfully, "this isn't one of those, I'm sorry to say."

"Oh."

"There she is," Tracker said, showing the man the tintype and watching his eyes. He saw very clearly that the hungry look in the man's eyes faded and was replaced by the furtive look an animal gets when it's been cornered by a larger predator.

Tracker guessed that was what *he'd* been all his life, a predator. It was a hell of a lot better than being the prey—which was what this bartender was, and he knew it.

The man looked at Tracker quickly, fleetingly, then down at the bar while he polished it with a damp rag.

"Nice," he said, "real nice."

"Yeah, but have you ever seen her?"

"Uh, no, I ain't, uh, never seen her."

"Oh," Tracker said, contriving to sound disappointed. "For a minute there, I could have sworn you had. I thought maybe you recognized her."

"No, no, I didn't," the man said quickly. "I didn't recognize her."

"Well. I thought you had," Tracker said, tucking the tintype away in his pocket. "Sorry you couldn't help."

"Yeah, so am I."

Tracker started toward the exit, as if to leave. Will Sullivan was seated at a table near the door and caught Tracker's nod. They would stay awhile.

Crystal Hale was walking a tightrope.

As the owner of the Crystal Palace she was perfectly aware of the fact that she owed money—and some sort of allegiance—to some unsavory Barbary Coast types. (She preferred to think of them in that way, rather than mention—or think—any names.) Yet, she had made an art of keeping them at arm's length for the past year. Sooner or later, though, she was going to have to make a choice between keeping her place, or giving herself over to them completely. And that meant Mannion.

The big man had made no secret of the fact that he wanted her. By stringing him along she had been able to buy what was now the Crystal Palace. He was becoming more insistent of late, however, saying that he would no longer speak or act on her behalf with...He never said who, but she knew.

She got up from her dressing table and walked to the full-length mirror on the inside of her closet door. She was tall—taller than most women—and full-bodied. Naked, she admired her own body with unabashed enjoyment. Her breasts did not sag at all, she was happy to see, even though she was nearly thirty-five. Her nipples were large and brown, her breasts full and round, her waist was still trim, her hips, thighs and calves still well-padded, but not overly so. She was a big woman, and that was part of her appeal to Mannion, who was a big man. That appeal was a cross it was becoming increasingly harder to bear.

She had finished "putting on her face" and now it was time to get dressed to go down and mingle with the customers. She only hoped that Mannion wouldn't show up tonight.

She had donned a gown of shimmering red when there was a knock at her door. It was the bartender, Jed, and he had something to tell her about a customer who was making him nervous. Mannion was usually the man who did that, but tonight it was someone else.

She went down to see who it was.

[9]

Tracker noticed the woman as soon as she got to the top of the stairway. He followed her progress down the steps and across the room, until he was sure she was heading his way. He'd expected someone to come and talk to him, because the bartender had become increasingly nervous about being watched, and had finally bolted from behind the bar and up the stairs.

"Enjoying yourself?" she asked when she reached his table.

"Very much," he answered, studying her with frank admiration. He was sure she was used to that.

She put her hands on her ample hips as if posing for him and asked, "Not gambling?"

"Oh, yes," he said, staring into her eyes, "I definitely am gambling."

She didn't understand the remark and frowned.

"May I join you?"

"Are we going to talk?"

"I think so."

"About what?"

"Oh, I don't—"

"Is there somewhere we could talk in private?"

She paused, studied him a moment and then a knowing look came over her face.

"Are you a policeman?"

"No, not a policeman."

She frowned.

"Are you from..."

"From where?" he asked. When she didn't answer he said, "Or should I say, from who?"

She realized her error and tried to cover it up, but the effort seemed halfhearted to him.

"Someplace private?" he repeated, breaking in on her thoughts.

She studied him again, head cocked to one side, and then said, "Come with me."

She started away and he stood up and followed, secure in the knowledge that Will was watching closely.

Upstairs, she took a key that hung on a ribbon around her neck from the deep V between her breasts and unlocked the door.

"Is this your inner sanctum?"

"That's exactly what it is," she said, opening the door. "I don't like anyone else to go inside when I'm not here. It's an intrusion."

"I'm honored by your invitation, then."

"You should be."

As she allowed the big man to enter, she admitted to herself that there was something compellingly attractive about him. If she had a choice between his turning out to be a cop or one of Mannion's men, she would have preferred that he be a cop. In actuality, though, she didn't believe that he was either one. He didn't look like a lawman, and he certainly didn't seem like the type of man who would work for Mannion.

She closed the door and then turned to face him with her hands on her hips.

"You're a lot of woman," he said frankly.

"And you're a lot of man," she said, matching his frankness with boldness.

"I guess that means we have something in common."

"I guess so."

"What's your name?"

"Crystal."

"As in Palace?"

"The same."

"I'm impressed."

"So am I."

"Should we talk, then?"

She hesitated, and then made a snap decision. Actually, it wasn't such a snap decision. It had been on her mind since she first laid eyes on him.

She walked up to him and said, "Why don't we get the obvious out of the way, first?"

He smiled and she crushed her breasts against him.

She was tall, he realized, even taller than he'd thought. He wrapped his arms around her, enjoying the feel of a big woman, and then their mouths were avidly crushed together, tongues lashing madly at one another.

Their clothes became obstacles, and they shed them quickly, helping each other. Her nipples were swollen and hard against his skin, scraping him, and her flesh was on fire, burning him. Her hands went between his legs; she was delighted with the long, swollen column of flesh she found there. She sank to her knees and caressed it between her large, firm breasts. Then, holding his cock by its base, she allowed it to slide between her full lips into the vacuum of her mouth.

Tracker's hands instinctively went to the back of her head as she sucked on him, moaning and trying desperately to accommodate his entire length. One hand hefted his balls as if they were a sack of jewels, while the other held the base of his penis tightly, forcing his orgasm to abate each time it threatened to burst from him.

"Jesus—" he said thickly, reaching down for her. He slid his hands beneath her arms and lifted her up from the floor with an ease that surprised her. She knew how big she was, and how much she weighed, and for him to lift her completely off the floor with such ease, he had to be an incredibly strong man.

Maybe even stronger than Mannion!

He turned quickly and deposited her on the bed, and then crouched between her legs to eagerly run his tongue along her oozing slit. It was her turn to grip his head tightly as he ran his tongue up and down, in and out, and finally focused his attention on her pleasure center. He sucked her clit between his lips and lashed it with his tongue until she was moaning and crying out, lifting her hips toward her impending orgasm. When it came she screamed, and he was glad that the noise downstairs was loud enough to drown her out.

"Oh, my God—" she gasped when she had gathered up enough breath to do so.

He rested himself on the cushion of her breasts, belly, hips and thighs and eased his swollen cock into her.

"Yes, yes," she said, as he went in deeper, inch by inch. "Oh God, oh Jesus, oh shit, yes..."

He moved rhythmically against her with long, hard strokes, and kept at it until her breath was rasping in her throat and tears were coming from her eyes. She had come several times already and as he felt her belly tremble with anticipation of another massive orgasm, he increased his tempo until he was spurting inside of her in long, powerful streams. She wrapped her legs around him and used her vaginal muscles to clutch and grasp at his cock, milking it dry while she moaned and babbled unintelligibly. She'd had a lot of men in her time—had been a whore for a lot of years before finally getting her own place—but she'd never had anyone like this man before. She'd never had anyone who could satisfy her incredible need and hunger for sex.

Now, she thought as the last spurt of his come emptied into her, she had found such a man, but she had no idea who he was!

Was he a fortunate find—for more reasons than one, she thought, thinking again of Mannion—or even more of a danger to her than anyone else?

"Now we get to the less obvious," she said a short while later, when they had both caught their breath. "Should we start with your name?"

"Tracker," he replied, idly twirling her pubic hair around his finger.

"Just Tracker?"

"Just Tracker."

Like Mannion, she thought, but she hoped that was the only similarity between them.

"Crystal, I showed your bartender something that scared him out of his wits."

"What was it?"

"Didn't he tell you?"

"He said there was a man downstairs that I should be aware of." She took his semierect penis in her hand and added, "He was right."

Tracker reached for his shirt, which had been thrown to the floor in their haste, and took the tintype out of his pocket.

"This," he said, handing it to her, "is what I showed him."

53

She took it and examined it, and then gave it back. He could have sworn it meant nothing to her.

"Do you know her?"

"No, I never saw her before. But..."

"But what?"

She hesitated, not knowing how much trouble she might be getting herself into. She had always known that the day would come when she had to make a choice. Maybe this was it, and maybe Tracker was the man to help her make it.

"She's a type."

"What type?"

"The type who gets bought and sold."

"On the white slave market, you mean?"

She was surprised that he had come up with that answer right away. She had expected him to think that she was talking about prostitution.

"Yes, but that's not a surprise to you, is it? Who are you, Tracker? Why did you come here?"

"I came here to the Barbary Coast, looking for this girl."

"Have you been to other places with this picture?" she asked then, with concern.

"Yes. Three others before here."

"Name them."

When he did she knew that at least two of them were controlled, and one had been backed, the way hers had.

"You might be in a lot of trouble, Tracker."

"With the Barbary Coast Tong?"

"You know about that?"

"Oh yeah. I was hoping to attract their attention."

Before she could reply there was a knock on her door.

"Who is it?"

"Sheila," came the reply.

"One of my girls," she explained, sliding off the bed to her feet and pulling on a robe. She walked to the door and opened it a crack. "What is it, Sheila?"

"He's downstairs," the girl said. "He wants to see you."

Crystal felt a chill and asked, "Mannion?"

The girl nodded.

"Tell him to wait."

She closed the door and turned to face Tracker.

54

"You said you were hoping to attract the attention of the Barbary Coast Tong?"

"That's right."

"Well," she said, hugging her arms to ward off a chill, "congratulations—you just may have."

[10]

"You want to explain that?" Tracker asked while she rushed him to get dressed.

"There's a man downstairs named Mannion who thinks he owns me."

"Mannion? What makes him think that?"

"It's a long story." She turned her back to him and said, "Would you?"

He secured her dress and then put his hands on her shoulders and said, "I've got time. I'm not going anywhere."

"Oh, but you have to go," she said, turning to face him and putting her hands on his chest. "If Mannion sees you—if he thinks that we—"

"But we did."

"He'll kill you!"

"You mean he'll try."

"No, you don't understand, Tracker," she said, and now her hands on his chest became fists. "Mannion is..."

"He's what?" She hesitated long enough for it to come to him and he asked, "Is he with the Tong?"

She pressed her lips together as if afraid that she might answer, but then nodded.

"Then he's a man I want to meet," he said, starting for the door.

"Wait!"

"What's wrong?"

Looking crestfallen she said, "Tracker, I have a confession to make."

"What?"

"When I saw you I thought you might be the man to...to handle Mannion and get him off my back, but

56

now I don't know. He's big and vicious, and he's an animal."

"And he's got the Tong behind him."

"Not here," she said. "He always comes here alone. He's been trying to get into my bed for a year, ever since the Tong fronted me the money to buy this place."

"For a percentage?"

"Yes. Mannion has been keeping them away from my door, but that means that *he's* always here, sniffing around me."

"He hasn't made it up here yet?"

She made a face and said, "He hasn't even come close, but I don't know how much longer I can hold him off."

Tracker trailed his index finger across her right cheek and said, "Let's go downstairs, Crystal."

"But Tracker—"

"Don't worry. Nothing's going to happen."

"I hope you're right," she said, looking dubious.

When Mannion saw Crystal coming down the steps with the tall man he froze. Immediately he recalled the leader's words to stay out of trouble when he wasn't on Tong business.

Well, he could always say he had come to collect.

When Crystal saw Mannion at the foot of steps, looking as huge and imposing as ever, the chill she had felt earlier came back, only this time it pierced her to the bone. She slowed down, but Tracker's presence behind her on the stairs kept her going. As capable as Tracker obviously was, she wondered if she wasn't going to have his death on her hands in a few minutes.

When Tracker saw Mannion he was impressed by the man's size, but he'd come up against large men before. His confidence in his own abilities had never wavered before, and it didn't now.

When Will Sullivan saw that the huge man at the foot of the steps was heading for a showdown with Tracker his first inclination was to get up and walk over to join them, giving Tracker some obvious support. He knew that Tracker wouldn't appreciate that, however. Besides, he had seen Tracker handle big men before.

Still, he tensed, ready to move quickly if the need arose.

"Who's he?" Mannion demanded.

Crystal and Tracker had reached the foot of the steps, and now that Tracker and Mannion were level with each other she saw that they were about the same height, but Mannion had a twenty-five or thirty-pound advantage.

Tracker noticed the weight discrepancy, too, but he didn't quite see it as a disadvantage for him.

"You must be Mannion," Tracker said, addressing the man.

"That's right."

"I'm Tracker. Why don't you ask *me* that question?"

Mannion moved his eyes from Crystal to the tall man with her, and Tracker noticed that the man had dead eyes, the color of mud. They were devoid of any expression, and he had his doubts about the man's intelligence. As it turned out, he might be the one with the advantage.

"Mister, this is my woman," Mannion said in a menacing, low tone so that only Tracker and Crystal could hear him.

"That's not the way I see it," Tracker replied, matching the other man's stare.

"I don't care how you see it," Mannion said, "I'm telling you the way it is. Crystal, you bitch—"

"Hey!" Tracker imposed himself between Mannion and Crystal. "That's no way to talk to a lady. If you've got something to say, say it to me."

They matched stares long enough for Crystal Hale and Will Sullivan to get nervous. Then Mannion said, "I've got plenty to say, but not here. Not now."

Mannion's huge fists were bunched at his sides, and the muscles on his shoulders and upper arms stood out. Tracker knew that the man would have liked nothing better than to take him apart at that moment, but something was holding him back.

"Why not?" Tracker asked, deciding to see if he could taunt the man into action. "What's wrong with now?"

"It's not the right time."

"We're both here. You afraid of being embarrassed in front of the lady?"

Crystal couldn't believe her ears. Why was Tracker deliberately baiting Mannion? Did he *want* to fight?

Mannion's face suffused itself with blood, but the man was able to restrain himself; Tracker wondered whether from loyalty to someone ... or from fear? Whatever it was, he had apparently been warned not to become involved in public brawls, because the man was obviously a brawler. The condition of his face—a previously broken nose, knotty scars—and his scarred knuckles attested to that.

"Mister, your time will come, believe me," Mannion finally said from between clenched teeth. He looked at Crystal and added, "Yours too, bitch."

He turned on his heel and stalked his way to the exit, brushing through people and almost knocking them down on the way. Tracker caught Will's eye and jerked his head, indicating that he wanted the ex-boxer to follow Mannion. He himself wanted to stay behind and talk to Crystal some more.

She just might be able to help him find Melody Tinsdale.

After Mannion had left, Tracker told Crystal he wanted to talk to her further.

"Upstairs?" she asked. Seeing Tracker force Mannion to back down had excited her, and she wanted to feel him between her legs again.

He smiled at her and said, "If we go upstairs, we're not going to get a chance to talk."

She grinned back at him lasciviously and said, "You're right about that. We could go back into my office."

"Let's do that."

"On one condition."

"What's that?" he asked, although he thought he already knew.

"When we're finished we go back upstairs." She moved closer to him and whispered, "I want to feel you inside me. I'm all wet—"

"All right," he said, interrupting her because if she

59

kept that up he'd drag her upstairs immediately. "We'll talk about that after."

"You want to come up, don't you?" she asked, moving closer to him. "You want to fuck me again, don't you?"

"Crystal," he said, "if we don't go into your office right now I'm not going to fuck you, I'm going you spank you, and in front of all these people."

"You wouldn't," she said, and it almost sounded like a dare. When he didn't reply she looked into his eyes and said, "I guess you would."

"I would."

"All right," she finally relented. "This way."

[11]

Will Sullivan hurried from the Crystal's Palace so that
Mannion wouldn't get too far ahead of him. Of course,
he hadn't been close enough to the conversation between Tracker and the other man to find out his name,
but Mannion's bulk was easy to spot as he walked hurriedly down California Street, brushing past the shills
and whores as if they didn't exist.

Once he spotted the man Will kept a respectable
distance, not wanting to give himself away. He was
quite a bulky man himself, however, and it wasn't hard
for Mannion to spot him.

Will Sullivan, ex—prize fighter, had no way of knowing that he was heading for his deadliest fight ever.

Mannion knew he was being followed, and he was
glad. He was going to get to take out his anger on
someone after all.

Making damn sure he didn't lose his tail, Mannion
turned into what he knew was a box alley, flattened
his back against the side of a building and waited. His
fists were balled up tight, and there was a tight grin
on his face. The only way this could have been better
was if the man behind him was Tracker; but he was
going to get to hurt somebody, and that was really what
counted.

He hadn't hurt anyone all day.

When Will turned into the alley his heart sank. It
was dark and he couldn't see. He was afraid he was
going to lose the man, and Tracker had been counting
on him.

He moved farther into the alley, away from the activity on California Street, moving slowly until his eyes adjusted to the darkness.

"Hey, friend."

The voice came from the darkness behind him.

"What?" he said, turning quickly.

"Keep moving along," the voice said. "I've got a gun trained on you. If you don't do what I tell you, I'll give you another belly button. Got it?"

"I got it," Will said. "Take it easy."

"Move."

Will groped his way down the alley until he found himself in a box, dimly lit by a lone streetlamp. He turned and saw the man he had been following facing him, empty-handed.

"What happened to your gun?"

The man grinned and said, "I don't need a gun, friend."

Very deliberately, the man removed his gun from his holster and tossed it into the darkness behind him.

"Mister," Will Sullivan said, "you just made a big mistake."

"My name's Mannion," the man said, "just so you know who's killing you." Mannion beckoned Will with his hands and said, "Come on."

"Will Sullivan," Will said, introducing himself.

When Will Sullivan had been in the ring he was a slugger, not a boxer. He was a take-two-to-give-one kind of fighter, and as he shuffled forward, fists at the ready, that was his game plan.

He moved in, waiting for Mannion to throw a punch, but the man just grinned at him. He looked as if he *wanted* Will to hit him, and Will finally decided that he had to oblige. A free shot would help get the fight over with, anyway.

Disdaining a jab to set the man up, Will decided to throw his best shot and brought his right up from the ground. It crashed into Mannion's face, forcing the man back a step—and that was it!

Will couldn't believe his eyes. The man had a bloody lip, but other than that the blow hadn't seemed to faze him. Will had knocked out over forty men with that punch, but Mannion just stood there, bleeding, and grinned at him.

"If that's the best you got," Mannion said, "this is going to be too easy."

"You gonna fight, or talk?"

Mannion laughed and moved toward Will. The ex-fighter threw a jab into Mannion's face, which bounced off, and then Mannion swung. As the blow struck Will in the face he knew he was in trouble, because he suddenly saw stars and staggered back several steps. He was stunned, but desperately tried not to show it. He swung his own right again, this time landing it just below Mannion's heart, a blow which should have damn well stopped his heart, but Mannion was proving to be more bull than man. He grinned at Will, and landed a blow of his own which cracked against Will's jaw, snapping his head back. His eyes failed at that moment, but he heard Mannion grunt and knew another punch was coming. There was nothing he could do to avoid it.

Will didn't know how much time had gone by, but the next time his eyes cleared he was sitting on the ground staring up at a smiling Mannion.

"Get up," Mannion said.

Will couldn't understand why the man hadn't simply stomped him to death while he was helpless, but he struggled to his feet. For the first time in his life he was in a fight he knew he couldn't win, and it was a frightening feeling.

For the first time in his life, he was afraid of another man!

[12]

"Tell me about this girl, Crystal," Tracker said, showing Crystal the tintype.

"I told you before that I didn't know her. I wasn't lying."

"Well, your bartender knew her. I'm sure of that."

"Not necessarily. He might have just recognized her type. Why are you so interested?"

"Her father is a very important man. He's hired me to find her. She disappeared a few days ago."

"I'll bet she either took off on her own, or with a guy. That's what I did when I was her age."

"How would you like her to go through what you went through?" Tracker asked, instinctively knowing that Crystal had led something of a hard life up to this point. Even now, when she had her own place, she still had to fear the Tong and men like Mannion.

Crystal stared at the tintype, tapping it against the palm of her left hand, looking thoughtful.

"I'll talk to him."

"Tonight?"

She shook her head.

"He won't talk tonight. Not after you and Mannion were here the same night."

"When?"

"Tomorrow, maybe," she said, handing the tintype back. "It will depend on how jumpy he is."

"I'll come back tomorrow night, then," he said, standing up, tucking the image of the girl away in his pocket.

"Hey," she said, rising from behind her desk, "what about tonight? Upstairs?"

Tracker faced her and said, "Get me some information on that girl, Crystal, and I'll spend a week with you upstairs."

"Will you keep me alive long enough to collect?"

"Mannion won't hurt you," Tracker said. "I'm going to pay him a visit, too—and his employer."

At the mention of the leader of the Barbary Coast Tong Crystal's expression turned apprehensive.

"Nobody's ever seen him."

"Then it's about time someone did, isn't it?"

When Tracker got back to Farrell House Deirdre was working the desk.

"Shana quit again?"

"No such luck," the blonde girl said. "No, she was notified a little while ago that something happened to Will."

"What?"

"Just before you got here the police arrived. They said they found Will in an alley on the Barbary Coast— wasn't he with you?"

"Where is he?"

"Sisters of Mercy Hospital. Duke went with her—" she said, but she was talking to thin air. She had never seen Tracker move so fast before.

Tracker found Duke sitting with Shana in the lobby of the hospital.

"Duke—" he said, approaching them.

Both Duke and Shana looked up at him and Duke stood up and moved away from Shana.

"What happened?"

"Somebody beat him half to death, Tracker, left him in an alley. He managed to stagger into the street where somebody saw him and called the police."

"Is he conscious?"

"He goes in and out, they say. They just got him here a little while ago. They think they can stabilize him, but whether or not he makes it is up to him."

"Where's the doctor?"

"In with him."

They were standing far enough away from Shana that she couldn't hear what they were saying.

"Shana—" Tracker started to say, but Duke put his hand on his friend's arm to stop him.

"She doesn't want to talk to you right now. She knows that Will was...working with you."

"He was only supposed to back me up, and then follow somebody. That's all he was doing, following a man named Mannion."

"I guess this Mannion saw him." Duke shook his head and said, "Tracker, I ain't never seen anybody as beat up as Will is. This Mannion must have had four or five guys work him over."

"I don't think so," Tracker said, thoughtfully. "I think he did it all by himself, Duke."

"One man did that to Will?" Duke asked in surprise. "Will was a pro—"

"This is a special man, Duke. He's going to take a special kind of killing."

Tracker threw a glance at Shana, whose face bore the tracks of many tears. She refused to look at him, and he swore he'd make it up to her and her brother.

"I'll see you later, Duke. See that he gets the best of care, I don't care how much it costs."

"All right."

Tracker started to leave but Duke stopped him again.

"You're going to need help."

"No," Tracker said. "That's what Will was doing. No more help, Duke."

Tracker looked back at Shana, and Duke said to him, "She'll be all right."

"Sure she will," Tracker said, "if he pulls through."

[13]

The following morning Chief Ansel Preston appeared at the hotel, asking to speak to Tracker. When Deirdre went to Tracker's room to inform him, he told her to put the chief in the dining room and give him whatever he wanted on the house. When he came down, Tracker found Preston there enjoying a huge breakfast.

"You must have considerable influence here," Preston said as Tracker joined him.

"Just coffee," Tracker told the waiter. As the man went to get it Tracker made a mental note to tell Duke to hire some waitresses. Give the customers something to look at while they eat.

"I'm just a permanent resident," Tracker said. "What can I do for you?"

"Seems a friend of yours got himself beat up last night," Preston said. "I'm here to ask you if you know anything about it."

"I might."

Preston stared at Tracker and said, "If you do, you'd better tell me."

"I might," Tracker repeated, "if I think the need arises."

Preston put his knife and fork down and stared hard across the table at Tracker.

"Look, Tracker, don't go taking the law into your own hands, not in my town. If you know who beat up Will Sullivan, tell me and I'll take care of it."

Sure, Tracker thought, all I've got to tell you is that a muscleman for the Barbary Coast Tong did it; you'll start shaking in your boots and back off immediately.

In any case, Tracker couldn't say with all honesty that he knew who did it. He suspected Mannion, but

67

Preston wasn't asking for his suspicious, but for what he *knew*.

"All right," Tracker said, as the waiter brought his coffee, "I don't know who did it."

Preston frowned, then picked up knife and fork and started eating again.

"You think you know, though, don't you?"

"I won't tell you what I think, Preston, only what I know—or, what I don't know. And I don't know who beat up Will Sullivan."

"Very well," Preston said. "This breakfast is excellent. You should try some."

"I'm not hungry."

"No, I don't suppose you are, not with your friend in the hospital in the condition he's in."

"You have word on his condition?"

"Only that the doctors say that he might never wake up."

"That means there's a chance he will."

"Yes, I suppose it does."

Tracker sipped the coffee, scalded his mouth and cursed. Preston looked amused, but said nothing.

"If that's all you want from me..." Tracker said, standing up.

"For now."

As Tracker turned to leave Preston called out, "Tracker."

"Yeah?"

"Thanks for breakfast."

Tracker almost said, "Anytime," but then decided that Preston might take him up on it.

"Don't mention it."

In the lobby Deirdre was once again at the desk. Tracker asked her when Duke had gotten back in.

"Late, but he's in the office now."

"Did he tell you about Will?"

"Yes." She studied his face and said, "You blame yourself, don't you?"

"Who else is there to blame?"

"What about Will? He didn't have to do whatever it was you wanted him to do."

"Sure. I'll be in the office with Duke."

"And after that?"

"Working."

That meant that she wouldn't know where he was, because he didn't even know.

Tracker stopped in the office just long enough to confirm what Preston had said about Will's condition.

"That's about right," Duke said. "The doctors said that all they can do is watch him very carefully. If he wakes up, he's got a good chance of pulling through."

"What about Shana?"

"I got her to go home, but she said she was going back early this morning."

"Go back over there and stay with her, will you, Duke? Don't leave her alone."

"Sure," Duke said, even though he'd intended to do that anyway.

"Send Dee a message if he wakes up. I'll want to talk to him."

"Will do."

"Get some temporary help for the saloon and the front desk."

"I'm already taking care of that."

Tracker nodded and headed for the door.

"Oh yeah, one other thing."

"What?"

"Hire some waitresses for the dining room."

Duke frowned and said, "Waitresses?"

"Yeah, waitresses. Women instead of men. The prettier, the better."

"All right, Tracker," Duke said, studying his friend intently, "all right. I'll take care of it."

"I'll be in touch."

"Be careful."

"Oh, sure."

As Tracker went out the door Duke was shaking his head. He'd never seen the big man so rattled. Briefly, he considered following him, but he knew that Tracker would spot him and wouldn't stand for it. He'd just have to wait to be asked for his help, and he hoped that what had happened to Will wouldn't keep Tracker from asking for it if he really needed it, that he wouldn't just go ahead and get himself killed before putting another friend in danger.

* * *

69

When Tracker exited the office Deirdre called out to him from the desk.

"What is it, Dee?"

"While you were in with Duke a small Chinese boy came in and left this for you." She was holding an envelope out to him with no name written on it. He took it and opened it.

It was a short note asking him to meet the writer at an address on Dupont Street in Chinatown. It didn't say when, and it didn't say why, but Tracker thought he knew why.

The note was from Anna Ching's brother, Lu Hom.

[14]

Since the note didn't specify a time, Tracker figured that meant any time would do. He decided to wait until after dark.

Leaving the hotel, he spotted one of Preston's men watching from across the street. First order of business was to lose him so that he wouldn't follow Tracker.

From Farrell House he went to California Street. He wanted to talk to Crystal Hale again and see if she could tell him where to find Mannion. He stopped first in a cafe and asked for the back door; leaving the lawman behind was as easy as that.

The Crystal Palace was closed, but he pounded on the front doors until the bartender appeared to open them.

"We're closed."

"Tell her I'm here."

"We're closed," the bartender said again and started to close the doors. Tracker lowered his shoulder and rammed it into the doors with all his weight behind it. The door struck the bartender solidly, sending him reeling back. He lost his balance after several steps and fell heavily onto a table which shattered beneath his bulk.

Tracker stepped inside, closed the doors behind him and locked them. He started across the floor toward the stairs and the bartender cringed on the floor, as if he thought Tracker were going to kick him. He breathed a sigh of relief when the big man walked right past him and up the steps.

When Tracker reached Crystal's door he knocked once and then impatiently opened it and walked in. He stopped short at what he saw in the bed.

Crystal sat up, staring at him in surprise. The sheet

fell away from her, revealing her naked breasts, nipples distended. Next to her in the bed was another girl who was also naked. Her breasts were smaller, but her nipples were in the same condition.

"Tracker!" Crystal finally said, throwing off her surprise. She seemed at a loss for a moment as to how to handle the awkward situation, but then he could see by the expression on her face that she'd adjusted to it. She stood up, pulled on a robe and then faced him.

"Well, darling, you've discovered my secret vice." She looked at the girl in the bed, who had decided to hold the sheet up against her breasts, covering them. She was pretty, and couldn't have been more than nineteen. She had dark hair and a small, heart-shaped face.

"I really don't care about your secret vices, Crystal," Tracker said. "I came to talk to you."

"This doesn't shock you?"

"Listen, if I didn't have something to do I'd join the two of you, right now, but I just don't have the time. Would you get rid of her, please?" He didn't wait for her to respond. He looked at the girl on the bed and said, "Look, honey, have you got your own room?"

"Y-yes."

"Well then, go to it, will you? You can come back and play later."

He walked to the bed and took her by the arm, exerting just enough pressure to force her to get up. He pushed her out into the hall naked and closed the door behind her.

"I hope she won't get embarrassed."

"Not at all," Crystal said, opening her robe again and letting it fall to the floor. "All of us women walk around naked all the time."

"I can believe it." He walked over to her, picked up her robe and draped it around her. "I came to talk."

"Pooh," she said, thrusting out her succulent lower lip. "What about?"

"Mannion."

She frowned.

"Why do you want to talk about him? You handled him pretty well last night."

"Not as well as I thought. It seems a friend of mine had an accident last night, only it wasn't an accident."

He explained to her what had happened to Will Sullivan after he left the Crystal Palace to follow Mannion.

"And now you want to get your revenge? I told you he was dangerous, Tracker."

"Yeah, well, I've been known to be a little dangerous myself." He took hold of her upper arms and squeezed just enough for her to feel it.

"You're hurting me."

"I want to know where I can find Mannion, Crystal, and I don't have time to ask nice."

"That doesn't matter," she said, trying to pull herself free from his grip. "I don't know where to find him. The only time I see him is when he comes around here. God, I wouldn't want to find him, Tracker." She pulled harder and when he didn't let go she added, "I'd tell you if I knew."

Tracker stared at her for a moment, then released her and said, "Yeah, I guess you would."

She rubbed her arms in an attempt to start the circulation again and said, "Jesus, you've got a grip like iron."

"Sorry."

"You're disappointed."

"Slightly."

"Can I make you feel better?" she asked, shrugging the robe to the floor again.

"Yes," he said, laying a finger alongside the nipple of her right breast, "see if you can locate him for me."

"Is that all?"

"No," he said, opening the door, "if he comes around here again, send someone to the Farrell House off Portsmouth Square and leave a message at the desk."

She frowned and said, "Is that all?"

"That's all," he said, looking her up and down. He wished he had time to stay. "I'll send your little friend back in on my way out."

Tracker did not go back to Farrell House because he didn't want to have to deal with another cop tailing him. He found a saloon and stayed there until darkness began to fall, then made his way to Chinatown and found the address on Dupont Street.

He knocked on the door. The familiar eye slot opened and he stood still while he was studied.

"Who?" a voice asked from behind the closed door.

"Lu Hom." Once again the eye looked him over, then the little door closed, a bolt was thrown and the larger door was eased open.

"Come," a voice said from the dark interior, and Tracker stepped inside.

Immediately he recognized the odor of opium, and wondered if Lu Hom had gone back to the dens since last he'd seen him. The door closed behind him and he turned to look at the elderly Chinese man who had closed it.

"This way," the man said, walking past him and leading the way.

He followed the little man up a flight of steps and into the dens. He expected to find Lu Hom in one of the many cribs there, but instead the old Chinaman led him through the room to a door in the rear and said, "Enter."

Tracker stepped past the man, opened the door and stepped through. He found himself in a small room that could have been used as anything. There was a cot and a chest of drawers, and a wooden table that could have been used as a desk. At the table sat Anna Ching's brother, Lu Hom.

"You came, Tracker."

"I came."

"Sit."

The only place there was to sit was on the cot, so he walked over and sat on it.

"Would you mind telling me why I'm here?"

"You have heard about my sister?"

"Yes. I'm sorry."

"That's why you are here, because you are sorry. You would like to find her killer, would you not?"

"Yes."

"So would I. I propose that we work together."

Tracker was surprised and said so.

"Do not be. My motives are logical. Anna was asking questions about the Barbary Coast Tong. This is not a true tong."

"That's what I've heard."

"It is controlled by the *lo fan*. That is why I need you. I will be able to go where you cannot, and you will go where I cannot."

"Makes sense."

"Then you agree?"

"Why don't you ask Colby?" Tracker said. "I understand he and your sister were—"

"I do not want Colby, I want you."

"What's wrong with Colby?"

"He is *lo fan*."

"So am I."

"It is not the same," Lu Hom said, staring at Tracker without expression.

"That's almost a compliment."

Lu Hom didn't reply to that, he just continued to stare at the much bigger man. There was more than a foot difference between the two men, and probably about eighty pounds or so, but Tracker knew that Lu Hom was solid, and that he was a fighter. He had seen the smaller man in action, and wouldn't have wanted to bet on himself in a fight against him.

Lu Hom was a good man to have on your side.

"All right," Tracker said. "All right, it's a deal."

The division of labor was easy. Lu Hom would work Chinatown while Tracker continued to work the Barbary Coast. Tracker made sure that Lu Hom knew what Melody Tinsdale looked like, although he knew that the Chinaman would interest himself in little else than finding his sister's killer.

Tracker was now certain, however—thanks to Lu Hom's remark about the Barbary Coast Tong—that it would all amount to the same thing.

Before going back to the hotel from Chinatown, Tracker stopped off at the hospital. He was relieved to find that Shana was not there. He wasn't sure how she would have reacted to his presence, but more importantly it meant that she was getting some rest.

He spoke briefly to the doctor, who told him that Will Sullivan had not awakened yet. His condition was still the same. If he woke up within the next couple of days, chances were he'd be all right.

Did Tracker know who had done this to Sullivan?

"Yeah, I think I know, doctor."

The doctor, a fairly young man as far as sawbones went, stared at Tracker and said, "Somebody ought to do something about it."

"Somebody will, doctor," Tracker said. "Count on it."

[15]

Mannion had some new information for the leader, info that the man wouldn't like.

When the big man entered the leader's lair he saw the girl on her knees in front of the man, her head bobbing back and forth. The leader stared at him and smiled, removed one hand from the back of the girl's head long enough to wave him to a chair. He sat down and continued to watch as the girl sucked on the other man and from the way the leader tensed and the sounds that the girl was making, he knew that the other man was coming.

He had a raging erection himself, and shifted in his chair to try to alleviate the pressure.

"All right, Carla," the leader said. The girl stood up and Mannion couldn't help but stare at her dimpled, firm buttocks. She went through the curtained doorway of the partition that held the leader's bed, probably to await the man's further pleasure.

The leader put on a robe and sat behind his desk.

"What is it?"

"Our man watching Lu Hom has reported something."

"What?"

"He had a meeting with the big man from last night, Tracker."

The leader raised his eyebrows and said, "Interesting. Tracker should have been the man you put in the hospital last night, Mannion, not the other man."

"Yes, sir," Mannion said, knowing there was no use in arguing. If he had fought with Tracker in the saloon, the leader would have heard about it and criticized him for fighting in public. He knew he could not win with the man, and had given up trying a long time ago. He didn't mind, as long as he was paid well.

"What do you think they were meeting about?"

"I don't know."

"No, you wouldn't. I think perhaps you'd better see about getting rid of Lum Hom before Tracker. It should be easier. People get killed in Chinatown every day. I mean, look at what happened to his sister." The leader fixed Mannion with a hard stare and said, "Do you see what I mean?"

"Yes, sir. I understand."

"You can leave now," the leader said. He rose, looked toward his bed and added, "I have other matters to attend to." He started walking toward the partition, then turned and said, "I'm counting on you, Mannion. Colby, Lu Hom, and Tracker. Those three men can be... troublesome, if we let them."

"Yes, sir. I understand."

"Would you like to watch?"

"Uh, no, sir," Mannion said, knowing that he'd better leave. He stood up and said, "No, sir, I'll be going."

After Mannion had left, the man he knew as the leader approached the girl on the bed and said, "Now for something entirely new, Carla. You're going to find this very interesting."

As Tracker entered the hotel Deirdre came out from behind the desk and rushed up to him.

"Preston is in the office, and he's fuming," she said hurriedly.

"Is Duke there with him?"

"Yes. Preston said he wasn't leaving until he saw you. I can tell him you never came back, if you like."

"No," Tracker said, "I'll talk to him. Thanks, Dee."

Deirdre went back behind the desk and Tracker headed for the office. As he entered Duke was saying, "I'm sure he'll be back soon enough—"

"I'm back. What's the problem?"

Preston had been sitting and now he bounded out of his chair and faced Tracker, red-faced.

"I had a man on you today and you lost him."

"Maybe he lost me."

"Don't get cute, Tracker. I want to know where you went today, and I want to know *now*."

Tracker looked at Duke, and the look was enough. Duke stood up and said, "I'll be...outside."

Preston watched Duke leave; Tracker never took his eyes off the lawman. When Duke was gone Preston looked back at Tracker.

"Well?"

Tracker moved toward the desk and took the seat Duke had just vacated.

"Why should what I did last night interest or concern you, Preston?"

"I told you. My man—"

"Lost me," Tracker interrupted. "Take it out on him, not on me. I'm kind of big to lose, if your man knew what he was doing, don't you think?"

"Oh, don't worry," Preston said, "he's paying for it. Believe me!"

"Why did you have a man on me in the first place?"

"Don't play cute with me, Tracker. You're after whoever killed your Chink girlfriend—"

"See, that confuses me," Tracker said, cutting the man off again.

"What does?" Preston asked, with a frown.

"This should be just another Chinatown killing to you. Just another slant-eye. Why are you so interested?"

"It's my job to be."

Tracker pulled a face and said, "Now who's being cute, Preston?"

Preston stared at Tracker in annoyance for a few moments, then abruptly stood up.

"Like I said earlier, Tracker. Don't go out there thinking that you can do my job. You're not empowered, and you're not qualified."

"I'll remember that."

Preston tried to think of a parting line, failed, walked to the door stiffly, and left.

Tracker thought again about the question he'd raised to Preston, the one that seemed to have prompted him to leave. Why was he so interested in another Chinatown killing—and this one wasn't even white? Tracker was sure that Preston had ignored enough of those in the past.

What was so special about this one?

[16]

The next morning a rather petite and fragile-looking Chinese girl entered the hotel and asked at the desk for Tracker. Deirdre was on the desk and she stared at the girl for a few moments before replying.

"What is it in reference to, please?"

"I'm sure that will be between Mr. Tracker and myself," the Chinese girl said in perfect, unaccented English.

"I see. Well, you'd have to see Mr. Farrell before seeing Tracker."

"I'm afraid that won't do," the girl replied, "Miss—?"

"Long, Deirdre Long. I am the owner of this hotel."

"The owner?" the Chinese girl asked, arching her delicate eyebrows in surprise.

"One of them."

"Would you please just let Mr. Tracker know I'm here and that I'd like to speak to him. I'm sure he'll see me."

Looking the girl over—forced against her will to admit that she was lovely—Deirdre, too, was sure Tracker would see her. She tightened her lips and said, "Have a seat, please."

"Thank you."

Deirdre decided that her best bet was to go through the drill, anyway. Let Duke be the one to decide to alter it. She went to the office and entered without knocking. It was, after all, her office, too.

"Duke?"

He looked up from the paperwork spread over the desk and said, "Yes, Dee?"

He and Tracker were the only two men who called her Dee, and they each had their own way of saying it. When Tracker said it she got the chills, and when Duke said it she felt warm. There was an affection between her and Duke that was quite different from what she felt for Tracker.

"There's a girl here who wants to talk to Tracker."

"A girl?"

"A Chinese girl."

Duke, interested, put down the pen he was holding. "What does she want?"

"She wants Tracker, and I don't think she'll talk to anyone else."

Duke frowned. Seemed a lot of people were feeling that way of late. They were going to have to change their drill, it seemed. He couldn't very well screen Tracker's visitors if they wouldn't talk to him.

"Well," he said, rising, "in light of the fact that she's Chinese—"

"And lovely," Dee added, ruefully.

Duke raised his eyebrows and said, "That, too. I guess I'll let the man know. Did he come down for breakfast, yet?"

"No."

"I'll go up and tell him. Entertain her, will you?"

"Oh, sure."

Deirdre went back behind the desk while Duke ascended the steps and made his way to Tracker's room. He was about to knock on the door when it opened and he was almost bowled over by the bigger man.

"Whoa!" he said.

"Duke. What's the matter?"

"Somebody downstairs to see you, Tracker. A lady."

"What kind of lady?"

"A Chinese lady," Duke said, figuring that would do the trick.

"Really?" Tracker said, with interest. "She say what she wanted?"

"Just that she will talk only to you. In light of recent happenings I thought—"

"You thought right," Tracker said, stepping back into his room. "Bring her up here, will you, Duke?"

"Sure."

"Who was on the desk when she came in?"

Duke smiled and said, "Deirdre."

82

Tracker closed his eyes and said, "It would be. I'll hear about this."

"I'm afraid so. I'll bring her up."

Tracker closed the door and looked around the room. It was decent except for the bed, but he didn't bother with that. He was sure that whoever the woman was, she had seen an unmade bed before.

He contained his curiosity about the Chinese girl until Duke arrived with her in tow.

"Tracker," Duke said at the open door, "this is Miss—"

The girl made a half turn toward Duke and said, "Thank you, Mr. Farrell."

Duke, at a loss, shrugged and backed away, giving Tracker a wry look.

"Come in," Tracker told the girl. She moved—or glided—past him and he shut the door and turned to examine her, aware that at the same time he, in turn, was being examined.

This girl looked nothing like Anna Ching. She was small, barely five feet tall, small breasted, but exquisitely formed. Her face was lovely, heart-shaped with slanting eyes, a smaller and broader nose than Anna's had been, but on this girl it was just right. The only resemblance between the two Chinese girls was the curtain of long, midnight black hair, but where Anna's part had been off center, this girl wore it right down the center. When the girl used her right hand to sweep her hair back over one shoulder Tracker noticed that she wore several rings.

"How do I stack up?" she asked, first to break the silence.

"What's your name?" Tracker asked, ignoring the question.

"I guess it's time for that, isn't it?"

"I usually prefer my visitors to be announced before I see them," Tracker said. "The time for your name was downstairs, but I'll take it now."

Her bee-stung mouth broadened into a smile and she reached into her small drawstring purse and came out with some identification, which she handed to the big man. Tracker read it with unconcealed surprise.

"Helen Chow," he said, handing the ID back, "Pinkerton operative."

"That's right," the girl said, replacing the identification in her bag. From the apparent weight of the small bag—and the fact that she was a Pink—Tracker was sure that there was also a small gun in the bag.

"Allan Pinkerton must be getting desperate," he said, deliberately testing her self-control.

She smiled again and said, "Please don't try to bait me, Mr. Tracker—"

"Just Tracker."

"I suppose you should call me Helen, then," she said, "since we're going to be working together."

"Is that so?"

"I hope so. I was sent here to approach you with the idea."

"Well, you approached me," Tracker said, "and unless you've got something else to say, I've got a big day ahead of me."

"It's not that easy, Tracker—"

"Sure, it is."

"Well, it shouldn't be."

She looked around for a place to sit and finally decided on the unmade bed.

"I've been sent here to work on breaking the white slavery ring that is apparently operating on the Barbary Coast," she said, running her hand over his sheets absently.

"Is that a fact? All by yourself?"

"Unfortunately, this is a busy time for the Pinkertons and a second operative was not available to accompany me. That is why Mr. Pinkerton suggested I approach you."

"He suggested that himself? I don't even know the man."

"He knows you—or rather, he knows of you. You were highly recommended as a competent man."

"I never thought of myself as fitting the mold of a Pinkerton man."

"Nor does he. His exact words were 'I'd never hire such a man, God knows, but he might be of considerable help to you in this instance.' I hope you will be."

"Oh, I'll be of considerable help, all right. I'll give you some advice—"

She stood abruptly before he could follow that up, smoothing down the front of her ankle-length skirt—but not before Tracker noticed that her legs and thighs were as exquisitely shaped as the rest of her.

"Advice is the last thing I need from you," she said hurriedly. "I really don't have time to convince you that I am a competent operative, Tracker. I'll merely point out the obvious reasons that I am qualified for this assignment."

"You're Chinese."

"Yes, that is certainly one of them," she agreed. "I will be able to move about freely in Chinatown and, to some extent, on the Barbary Coast."

"How are you at being a whore?"

"I beg your pardon?"

"That's the only way you'll be able to move about the Barbary Coast," he explained, "and even then, it won't be easy."

"I am used to difficult assignments. When you are a woman, and Chinese, they are all difficult to some degree."

"Yeah, I suppose they are," Tracker said, thoughtfully. "I'll tell you what. I'll get you a room here in the hotel so you can freshen up, and then we'll discuss it over dinner this evening."

She frowned and said, "I'd hoped to get started before then."

"This is the best I can do," Tracker said, spreading his hands in front of him, "unless you'd rather just work alone."

"I could," she assured him, "but it wouldn't be the smart thing to do."

"Let's go downstairs and get you that room, then."

"Very well," she said, moving toward the door, "I could use a bath."

As she passed him he caught her scent and admitted to himself that this woman interested him—and aroused him. For a fleeting moment he wished he could just take her, tuck her in his pocket and forget about everything else.

That, however, wouldn't be the smart thing to do.

When Tracker took Helen Chow downstairs and told Deirdre to check her into a room, his blonde partner arched an eyebrow at him and asked, "On the same floor as you?" with an innocent look on her face.

Tracker gave her a hard look and said, "Wherever there's room, Dee."

"Of course."

Having given the Chinese girl over to Deirdre's care, Tracker sought to excuse himself.

"Couldn't we talk now?" Helen Chow asked quickly, placing her hand on his arm in a restraining gesture. For the first time she was exhibiting something less than total confidence and icy—and inscrutable—calm.

"This evening," Tracker said again, "at dinner. By that time I should know whether I want to work with you or not." Tracker looked at Deirdre then and said, "Take good care of her, Dee."

"But of course."

[17]

Tracker went to the office to explain to Duke just who and what Helen Chow was.

"A Pink?" Duke asked in disbelief. "That little girl?"

"That little girl," Tracker said, "but I'd like to check with the Pinkertons in Chicago and make sure she's for real."

"I can take care of that."

"I was hoping you'd say that. See if you can get me an answer today, will you?"

"I'll give it my best shot. There may be one or two people in Chicago that I can use."

"Good. I'll see you later."

"Where are you off to?"

"I'm going to try a different trail than the one I've been following," Tracker said, and left.

It was time to see if a certain diamond had suddenly found itself on the market—and if it had, John Cooper would be the man who would know.

John Cooper had come to San Francisco after Tracker and set up shop on Kearny Street. Ostensibly running a gunsmith shop, he actually dealt in stolen goods, buying and then selling at a considerable profit. Jewelry was not quite his line, but if a diamond such as Tinsdale's had suddenly become available, he'd hear about it.

"Tracker, welcome to my shop," Cooper said as the big man walked in.

"Looks good, Coop," he said, looking around. "Where do you keep the other stuff?"

Cooper smiled—not a pretty sight. He was perhaps the ugliest man Tracker had ever met, yet he never seemed to want for female companionship. Like now.

The girl who came out from a doorway at the back of the shop was tall, slim and blonde, and when he saw her Cooper smiled again. Tracker assumed that the man's ugliness must have been a challenge to women, like a bull and a red flag.

"This is Terry," Cooper said. "Terry, meet an old...acquaintance," the man said. "This is Tracker."

"Hello," she said, her voice deep and throaty. "I'm going to do some shopping, honey."

"Sure, babe. Got enough money?"

"Always," she said, kissing his cheek. "Nice meeting you," she said to Tracker on the way out. He didn't have time to answer.

"What brings you here?" Cooper asked. He was a tall, dark-haired man in his thirties and if it wasn't for his incredible homeliness he would have looked like anyone else.

"A diamond."

"Buying or selling?"

"Looking for."

"Where's it from?"

"Can't say, but it would have hit the market recently."

"Who had it?"

"A girl, a young girl."

"Was she selling?"

"I don't know, Coop. The fact of the matter is they're both missing, and the last time they were seen they were together. It doesn't have to be that way now."

"I understand. What's she look like?"

"I don't know," Tracker said. "What's a diamond look like, a rock? It's probably round—"

"I meant the girl."

"Oh, the girl, sure." Tracker took the picture out of his pocket and showed it to Cooper.

"Pretty," Cooper said, "and dangerous."

"What do you mean, dangerous? How?"

"How is a woman dangerous?" Cooper said, handing the picture back.

"How can you tell by looking at a picture?"

Cooper shrugged and said, "I know women."

"What about diamonds?"

"I haven't heard anything of late," Cooper said, and Tracker believed him.

"All right. If you do hear anything I'd appreciate you letting me know."

"Still at the Farrell House?"

"Still there."

"It's a nice little hotel, but why don't you move into something in the square?"

Tracker grinned and said, "There's something homey about the Farrell House. When I'm there I just feel like it's mine."

He made a few more stops that day, leaving word that he was interested in a diamond, but none of the others he saw had earned his confidence the way that John Cooper had by his past deeds. The others were people he had met since he came to San Francisco. Once he had decided that he would stay and spend his time between jobs in the large city, he started to move around and get to know the kind of people he could possibly make use of in his line of business, which was recovery.

When he returned to the hotel in the late afternoon Deirdre was still on the desk.

"Can't you get someone to cover for you?" he asked.

"Why? You have something in mind?"

"The only thing I have in mind is your not working yourself to death."

"It's my hotel—our hotel, excuse me—and I can work myself to death if I want to."

"Heard from Shana?"

Deirdre relaxed and became serious and said, "No change in Will's condition. She must be going out of her mind."

"Well, she's got friends," Tracker said. "You and Duke do what you can for her."

"What about you?" Deirdre asked, not believing her own ears.

"I doubt that she wants anything to do with me right now," Tracker said, "and maybe never again."

"It wasn't your fault, Tracker."

He didn't reply.

"What did you do with Helen Chow?"

Deirdre's face tightened up again and she said, "Your

new Chinagirl is on your floor. I figured I'd make it easy for you."

"Pull in your claws, girl," he said, and his tone of voice made her straighten up and stare at him. "Where is she?"

"Upstairs in her room."

"I want to know if she leaves the hotel. If she does, find me right away."

"All right. What's going on?"

"Just do what I tell you, Dee. I appreciate it."

He walked past her toward the office and she watched him with a puzzled look until he went through the door.

"You're back," Duke said from behind the desk.

"What did you find out?"

"Your friend's name *is* Helen Chow and she *was* a Pinkerton operative at one time."

"Was?"

"Not anymore. Old Allan let her go. Seems her methods were a bit too radical for his taste."

"So if he didn't give her my name, who did? And what is she really up to?"

"You're asking the wrong person."

"Right," Tracker said, "and it's time to ask the right one."

[18]

When Helen Chow answered her door she was wearing a long, voluminous dressing gown with Chinese characters on it. Tracker had no idea what they said, if anything. The gown effectively hid her figure, and if he hadn't already known how shapely she was, he wouldn't have been able to guess.

"I've been expecting you," she said, backing away so as to allow him to enter.

"For dinner?"

"I'd much rather have some conversation."

"So would I. For openers, you don't work for Allan Pinkerton anymore. He didn't like your style."

"He's too old-fashioned," she said with disdain. "You checked up on me, huh?"

"Didn't you expect me to?"

"I'd have been disappointed if you hadn't. You must have some questions."

"A lot."

She sat herself down on the edge of the bed, crossed her legs and said, "Ask."

It was a little difficult to concentrate with her sitting like that, because she was leaning forward just enough to make the front of the gown gape. What he saw were two small, perfectly formed breasts, but he couldn't quite make out her nipples. He found himself leaning forward trying to catch a glimpse of what *color* they might be. Coral pink? Copper?

"Tracker?"

"Yes?"

"You have some questions," she reminded him, grinning. She knew what he was trying to do, and she made no effort to lean back and change the view. Neither did she lean forward more.

"How did you get my name?"

"From a mutual friend."

"Who?"

"I'd rather not tell you that right now."

"Why?"

"I still want you to help me, but not because, uh, he sent me to you."

Tracker frowned. Whatever she wanted she could probably have gotten it a lot easier by mentioning their friend's name. This girl wanted him to help her, but she didn't want him to feel obligated to.

"All right, let's set that aside for now," he said. "What are you doing here? What is it you want my help with? I don't want to stand here asking questions all night, girl, so just tell me what it's all about."

"It's simple," she said, standing up. When she did that her figure again disappeared within the folds of the gown. "You already know that I've been fired by Allan Pinkerton. What you don't know is that I'm damned good at what I do."

He could have guessed.

She paced the room with quick, nervous strides, not because she was nervous, but because she was a bundle of excess energy.

"I want to set up my own office, Tracker. I don't know where yet—it could even be here in San Francisco— but before I do I've got to do something big, make a name for myself."

"By busting up the white slavery business on the Barbary Coast."

"Right," she said, whirling on him, "but I don't know this city. I don't know the Barbary Coast."

"And I do?"

"Yes. I'm smart enough to know when I need help, Tracker. I'm in a strange town, and I need help. Your help."

"Helen—if that's your name..."

"It is," she said, smiling fleetingly.

"Helen, I haven't lived here all that long. I don't know the whole city, myself."

"But you know people. A man in your business—"

"What do you know about my business?"

"It's very close to mine," she said. "You recover things

for people for half of their value. I sometimes get paid to recover things, sometimes I get paid for other kinds of cases. We could work together, Tracker—"

"If you were given my name by a mutual friend, then you know I work alone."

"Basically, you do. So do I, but sometimes we have to bring in other people, to help."

Yeah, he thought, and sometimes those people get hurt...like Will Sullivan.

"Tracker, I'm not asking you to be my partner, I'm asking you to help me just this once."

"I'm working on something now—"

"Something that has to do with the Barbary Coast?"

"As it happens, yes. It might also be connected with the white slave thing."

"You know who runs it?"

"Talk is it's controlled by something called the Barbary Coast Tong."

"I've run across that name in my preliminary investigation. It's supposed to be run by Caucasians, isn't it?"

"That's right."

"Well, this is perfect, then. We're already working on the same case. By working together we can bust it up even faster."

Why not? Lu Hom was working Chinatown, Tracker had the word out on the diamond. What he really needed to do was find Mannion, and maybe Helen Chow could help with that.

"All right," he said, "we'll work together." He moved toward her and held out his hand for a handshake.

"Oh," she said, "I think we can think of a better way than that to seal this bargain."

She shrugged her shoulders and suddenly the robe was in a heap at her feet.

He was frozen by her beauty. Her breasts were very round and would barely fill his hand. Her nipples were coral pink after all, and already distended. Her stomach was very flat, while her hips flared outward, perhaps larger than they should have been for a woman of her size, but he wasn't about to complain.

She seemed to sense his fascination with her and she proceeded to execute a slow pirouette so that he could see all of her. Her buttocks were round, perfectly formed—naturally—and firm-looking. Her legs were smooth and muscular, her skin pale and without blemish.

"What is it?" she asked. "Is it because I'm Chinese? Haven't you ever had a Chinese girl?"

"One," he said. "That's not it. I'm fascinated by your...size."

"And I by yours," she said. "Are you that large...all over?"

"Are you sure you won't break?" he asked.

She smiled and approached him. She put her hands over the large bulge in his pants and said, "Don't worry, Tracker. I won't break. Mmm," she said, rubbing him through his trousers, "You are that large all over."

He started to lean over to kiss her, but sensed that he'd either end up with a sore neck or a twisted back.

"There must be a simpler way to do this."

"There is," she said, unbuttoning his shirt. She ran her hot tongue over his bare chest and said, "We need to be lying down."

"That sounds good."

"But first you have to remove all of your clothes," she said, pulling his shirt open further. "And quickly."

"Wait for me on the bed," he said, "and I'll be right with you."

He watched as she turned down the bed and lay down on her side, waiting for him. She scratched the inside of her left thigh with the toes of her right foot and he was fascinated again, this time by the play of muscles in her right leg.

"Clothes," she said.

"Right."

She watched with pleasure as the big man undressed. He was easily the largest man she would ever have been in bed with—in more ways than one—and she was anxious to get started.

She enjoyed the way he moved, so graceful for one so large. Finally he was naked and she could not take her eyes from his huge erection. It was pulsating, as if it had a life of its own, and as he approached the bed she took it in both of her small hands, unable to accommodate its entire length. She leaned forward and lov-

94

ingly ran her tongue over the bulbous head, wetting it with her saliva, and finally she allowed it to slide between her lips. Little by little she began to take more and more of him into her mouth, and they were both surprised at how much she was able to accept.

"Helen...Jesus," he said, taking her head in his hands. Her long black hair had fallen over her face and he could no longer see his cock disappearing into her mouth, but he could feel it! The girl was incredible! He briefly remembered asking her if she had ever worked as a whore, and wondered...

She moved one of her hands so that she could cup his balls and caress them gently. She allowed his cock to escape her mouth, and then began to lick the entire length of it up and down. He ran his hands over the smooth skin of her back, found her vertebrae and traced their path with his fingers. He worked his way down to the cleft between her cheeks and she spread her legs so that he could find her cunt. She was such a small girl that he was able to slide his middle finger into her while she was still sucking on him. She began to move her buttocks in a circular motion, grinding herself down on his finger.

"Jesus..." she said suddenly. "Come on the bed with me. Hurry, hurry, put it in me."

He removed his finger from her and she laid down on her back, legs open wide for him. He climbed onto the bed with her, but instead of driving his saliva-slickened shaft into her he ducked his head and began to lick her pussy with his tongue.

"Oh, God, yes," she said, cupping the back of his head with her hands. "That's it, that's it...oh, Jesus!"

She cried out as he found her swollen love bud and took it between his lips. He alternately sucked on it and manipulated it with his tongue and suddenly she was pushing her crotch tightly against his face saying, "Yes, dammit, yes, suck it, suck it hard, I'm...Jesus, I'm coming..."

He sucked on her until her spasms passed and then he straddled her and drove his pulsing shaft deeply into her.

"Ohhh..." was all she could manage as she wrapped

her small legs around him and began to beat her tiny fists against his back.

He reached beneath her and cupped her small, firm buttocks in his hands and pulled her tightly against him. Her breasts were like two hard peaches pressing against his chest.

"Christ, you're splitting me apart!" she cried out.

"Am I hurting you?"

"No, dammit, I told you I won't break. Just keep doing it, Tracker. I love it!"

So did he. He squeezed her buttocks tightly, knowing that he was hurting her, but she seemed to enjoy that as much as anything else. Her nails were raking his back now and her breath was just a rasp in her throat.

"Tracker, wait, please—" she said suddenly.

"What is it?"

"I want it from behind. I want you to do me like a dog. Please."

"Whatever you want."

He withdrew from her and she quickly got to her knees and presented him with a pulse-pounding view of her behind. He spread her cheeks, exposing her little brown hole, and his engorged penis, slick with her juices, slid into her very easily.

"Oh, yes, that's it," she cried. "Now pound it into me, as hard as you can."

He proceeded to do just that, holding her by the hips and driving the length of himself in and out of her while she moaned and cried and laughed. Helen Chow took great joy in sex and, although she would apparently try anything, she had definite preferences.

He released one of her hips because there was no further need for him to hold her. She was driving her butt back into him in time with his thrusts, and he freed one hand to reach around her and sink a couple of fingers into the steamy depths of her slick pussy. With his thumb he found her swollen clit and began to manipulate it while fucking her from behind. The dual stimulation quickly drove her over the edge and she screamed as she climaxed the first time. He did not slow his thrusts, however, and quickly drove her to a second climax, and this time he joined her.

"Oh God, I can feel you coming inside me," she cried.

"It's so hot, it's so good! I want it all, Tracker, I don't want you to ever stop."

Her muscles tightened around him to illustrate her words, and she seemed to be milking him for every drop that he had to offer—and more—but finally he was empty and ready to withdraw.

"No, don't pull it out," she said quickly, her tone almost pleading. She clenched her muscles again and added, "I want to feel that big, hard cock of yours go soft inside me."

Tracker still had two fingers inside her cunt and now he wiggled them around and said, "I think the opposite might just happen, Helen. If I don't get out now I may never get soft again."

"That's fine with me, Tracker," she said, wiggling her butt enthusiastically. "This is one hell of a way to seal a bargain, isn't it?"

He couldn't argue with that.

Tracker begged off from having dinner with Helen Chow—and then returning with her to her room—because he didn't want to flaunt the Chinese girl in Deirdre's face. He told Helen that he had some things to check on which precluded their having dinner together, but that he would see her later.

"We have plans to make," she reminded him.

"Yes, I know," Tracker assured her, "and we'll make them, but I've got a few things to do first."

"Don't forget me," she said, giving him a seductive look.

"How could I do that, Helen?"

"You might force yourself," she said, and the look she was giving him changed subtly.

"Helen, you wound me," Tracker said, pulling on his boots. "I said we had a bargain and we sealed it, remember?"

"*I* remember," she said pointedly.

"And so do I," he assured her, standing up.

"Come back later," she said, stretching on the bed so that he could see every inch of her splendid body. He knew she was trying to use her obvious charms to her best advantage, and he couldn't very well blame her for that. You did the best you could with what you had.

And Helen Chow had quite a bit.

[19]

Tracker went to the Barbary Coast.

He wanted to make one last try at finding Mannion on his own before using Helen Chow. He liked the girl, liked her determination, but she was still an unknown quantity. He didn't want to risk using her on Mannion because she might end up getting hurt.

He went back to the Crystal Palace, hoping that Mannion might put in an appearance there. He checked in with Crystal to see if the man had been back since that night.

"No, thank God," she said, "but I expect him to show up again. He's not going to let me go unpunished for that evening."

"Don't worry about being punished—"

"Yeah, I know," she said, interrupting him, "you'll protect me. That's fine if you're here, but what happens when you're not?"

She had a point.

"I'm going to try and make sure he never comes back here, Crystal, regardless of whether I'm here or not."

"First you've got to find him."

"Well, I'm going to sit here for a while and see if he shows up."

They were conversing at the base of the steps, and she said, "Well, if you get tired of sitting down here you're welcome to come upstairs."

At that moment a girl came walking down the steps and he recognized her as the pretty one who had been in bed with Crystal when he interrupted them.

"I wouldn't be interrupting anything, would I?"

"Not while you're around," she said. She put her hand on his arm and said, "Ah, that didn't put you off, did it? I mean, you didn't seem shocked—"

"When this is all over," he said, "I'll come back and show you how two beautiful women in one bed puts me off."

"I'll hold you to that."

He watched with enjoyment as she walked up the steps, and then when she was out of sight he picked out a corner table and settled down with a mug of cold beer to wait. The room was crowded and he was sure that, even though he was alone, he was fairly inconspicuous. While he could see the door clearly, those entering didn't necessarily have a good view of Tracker.

A couple of hours passed, during which Tracker had risen once to get a fresh beer. When it seemed clear that Mannion wasn't going to show up, Tracker briefly considered taking Crystal up on her invitation, but the session with Helen Chow had pretty much drained him, and although he did feel like going to bed, all he had on his mind was sleep.

He drained his mug and headed for the door—unaware of what was waiting for him outside.

When Tracker entered the Crystal Palace the man standing in a darkened doorway across the street straightened abruptly. He'd been standing there for hours waiting for just this moment. He backed up, felt for the doorknob behind him and opened the door. Inside there were three other men, all Caucasians, all members of the Barbary Coast Tong.

"Wake up, dammit," he snapped, nudging each man in turn, none too gently. His annoyance stemmed from the fact that they were sleeping and he was not. They had all agreed to draw high card for the watch rather than sharing it, and he had lost.

"Wha—" the other men said, each in turn, on awakening.

"Come on. He's across the street."

"Who?"

"Tracker. He's there."

Now the other three men shook themselves awake because it was time to go to work. Mannion had told each of them that if they didn't kill Tracker, they had better leave San Francisco and keep going. If they failed, each of them was prepared to do just that.

100

"He went in," the man on watch said. His name was Pronzini, and the other three men were Gores, Wilcox, and Hansen.

"Now all we've got to do is wait for him to come out," Gores said.

"Right."

They all moved to the front of the small store they had appropriated for this assignment, and stood looking out the window. When Tracker left they would see which direction he was taking, and then all four of them would run out the back door and prepare to greet him further down the street. His death was to be accomplished as quietly as possible, meaning they couldn't just open fire on him, which would have been the easiest way. If it was at all possible, however, Mannion wanted it to seem that the man had simply disappeared. This would not be the first such incident on the Barbary Coast. The police, and anyone else, simply would assume that the man had been shanghaied and was somewhere out at sea.

He'd be at sea, all right. After they killed him they'd weight him and dump him off the nearest dock, and that would be his eternal resting place.

Pronzini, intently staring out the window, suddenly heard the sound of a match being struck, then smelled smoke. He turned and hissed viciously at one of the men, "Put out that cigarette!"

When Tracker stepped onto the boardwalk in front of the Crystal Palace he took a deep breath. Out of the corner of his eye he thought he caught a flash of light in a window across the street but as he prepared to look again, the light was suddenly doused.

It had been there, however. Of that he was sure. But all the establishments across the street were closed, except for a couple of small saloons, neither of which was situated directly across from the Crystal Palace.

He started down California Street. To all appearances he seemed very relaxed, but in reality he was fully alert. His ears were open and his muscles were tensed.

This condition saved his life.

They came at him as he was passing an alley—the

very same alley where Will Sullivan had absorbed his beating at the hands of Mannion, although Tracker did not know that. He knew only that two men had stepped out of the darkened alley, and that two others had stepped from two separate doorways.

They all had their guns drawn, but as Tracker peered closely at them he saw that none of them had their weapons cocked, nor did any of them have their fingers on the triggers of their guns. Obviously, they were not prepared to shoot him.

"Just stand easy, mister," one of the man said. "One of my friends is going to take your gun from you."

"Not a chance," Tracker said.

"What?" one of the men said.

The first man who had spoken stared at Tracker and said, "Mister, in case you ain't noticed, there's four guns pointing at your belly."

"I noticed," Tracker said. Never a man particularly known for his speed with a gun—Tracker's talents lay in other areas—Tracker nevertheless drew his pistol and, as an object lesson, fired into the chest of that first man. The others, shocked by the action, watched their comrade as he staggered backward from the impact of the bullet, and then fell to the ground. While they were so occupied, Tracker turned and shot one of them as well.

"That's two down," he said to the remaining men, "and there's plenty of room on the ground for two more. Care to join them?"

Neither Gores nor Wilcox answered. Their guns were held low, uncocked, and both knew they'd never be able to bring them to bear on the big man in time.

"No? Good. Drop your guns, then, and let's take a walk before a crowd gathers—though God knows, it would probably take more than just two shots to draw a crowd around here." He cocked his gun to reinforce his command and said, "Drop 'em and let's move."

The two men dropped their guns and started to walk along the street. The three of them had melted into the darkness before anyone came along and discovered the bodies of Pronzini and Hansen.

* * *

"This is far enough," Tracker said.

"Here?" Gores said.

"Here," Tracker agreed.

They were on the docks, and this particular section was dark and empty at this time of night. Further along there were some well-lit docks, but they would not have served Tracker's purpose.

"I want to know where I can find Mannion," Tracker told them. He pointed his gun at the man named Gores and said, "You first."

"Who? I don't know anyone—"

"You," Tracker said, pointing his gun at Wilcox.

"I don't know no Mannion, friend. Listen—"

"Can you boys swim?"

"What?" they asked in unison.

"Swim, can you swim?"

"I hate the water," Wilcox said, and immediately realized that he'd made a mistake.

"Is that a fact? What about you?" Tracker said, asking the other man.

"Me? I can stay afloat..."

"Indefinitely?"

"Huh?"

"Jump in, both of you," Tracker said, jerking his gun toward the water.

"What for?" Gores asked.

"You're going for a swim."

"Listen, mister—"

"We're going to see how long the two of you can stay afloat."

"When can we get out?" Gores asked.

"When one of you tells me where I can find Mannion."

"Mister, we could drown—"

"And you will if I don't hear what I want to hear. You'll just keep treading water until you get too tired, and then you'll sink like a stone. I wonder which of you will go under first?"

"You can't—" Gores said.

"Sure I can," Tracker replied, taking a step forward. "Watch."

He planted his hand against the chest of Wilcox and

103

pushed. The man's arms flailed about uselessly and he tumbled off the docks into the water.

"You next," Tracker said.

"N-no, I c-can't swim—"

"That's tough."

Tracker reached out to give Gores a push, but Gores put his hands up in front of him and said, "Wait, wait."

"For what?"

"I gotta think," he said, conscious of the splashing sounds his friend was making in the water.

"Of a lie? I haven't got that much time. I need the truth."

"All right, all right," the man said as Tracker reached for him again. "Listen, he'll kill us—"

"H-hey—" the man in the water called, splashing around. "I-I can't—"

"Quiet," Tracker said to the man in the water, and then said to the other man, "Go ahead."

"I-I don't know where he lives, all I know is someplace he goes a lot."

"Not the Crystal Palace," Tracker said. "If you're going to tell me that, you might as well join your friend in the drink."

"No, no, it's not the Palace, it's another place. A Chinese whorehouse."

"In Chinatown?"

The man nodded and said, "In Ross Alley. He hates Chinamen, but he likes putting it to their women."

"That's all you can tell me?"

"That's all I know, mister, honest."

"Hey," the man in the water yelled, panic in his tone, "I'm drowning."

"If Mannion finds out I told you, he'll kill me."

"You better get out of town, then," Tracker said.

"That's what I'm gonna do."

"Yeah," Tracker said, "but after you save your friend."

"H-help!" came the call from the water.

"But I can't swim!" the man on the dock said.

"Learn," Tracker said, and pushed him in.

[20]

Ross Alley was a familiar place to Tracker, even though he hadn't been there in over a year. Ah Ching and the White Pigeon Tong had been headquartered there, before Lu Hom and Tracker broke it up.

It looked the same, dark and quiet. But Tracker knew the kind of action that was taking place behind the walls. Gambling, opium, and whoring. It was the latter that interested him at the moment, inasmuch as it interested Mannion.

There were several cribs on Ross Alley, but there was only one big whorehouse, and it was run by Miss Ting. Nobody knew what her full name was—or if they did, they weren't saying—so everybody simply called her Miss Ting. Tracker had heard of her, but had never met her. He was about to remedy that situation.

He knew where the entrance to the whorehouse was; now all he had to do was get through it. He had left a message with the old man at Lu Hom's office, but he couldn't afford to wait for the tough little man—he didn't have the patience.

He knocked on the door and, when the ever-present eyehole slot opened, he said the only thing he could think of that might get the door open.

"Mannion."

There was a pause—and he could see the indecision in the eye that was peering out at him—but finally the lock was pulled back and the door opened. The man who opened it was young, dark-haired, and skinny, and Tracker had no doubt that the man was dangerous, as well.

He had to play this right, or get into a dance with Miss Ting's chief bouncer.

"I would like to see Miss Ting."

"You said . . . Mannion."

"Is he here?"

"He is not."

"Is he expected?"

"I will take you to Miss Ting."

"Fine."

He followed the man down a long hallway into a large, well-lit room. This was different from any other such establishment in Chinatown. For one thing, Miss Ting offered all varieties of girls and not just Chinese. For another, you were virtually assured that they were clean. And for a third, from the way this main room looked, Tracker was sure that the beds would have clean sheets.

They walked through the room that was full of over-stuffed couches and crystal chandeliers to a door set in the back wall. When they went through that door they were in another hallway and Tracker had a funny thought that perhaps the man was simply leading him to the rear exit.

Finally they came to a door and the Chinaman knocked gently with the knuckles on the back of his hand.

"Come," a voice called from inside.

Tracker's guide opened the door and said, "A gentleman to see you, Miss Ting."

"Show him in."

The Chinaman looked back at Tracker and gestured for him to enter the room first. When Tracker did, the man entered behind him, closed the door and stood with his back to it.

Miss Ting sat behind a desk and regarded Tracker quizzically. She was Chinese, but beyond that Tracker couldn't tell much. She was the kind of woman who could have been thirty or fifty or anywhere in between. Her black hair was piled high up on her head with what appeared to be diamonds placed here and there. None of them—if they were real—seemed large enough to be Tinsdale's.

"You wanted to see me?" she asked.

Tracker turned and stared pointedly at the man standing at the door.

"That is Lee. You may speak in front of him. In fact, you will have to."

"Fine," Tracker said. "I'm looking for a man named Mannion."

"Do you want to kill him?" she asked anxiously.

"I want to find him. I understand he comes here often."

"Yes," she said, her face wrinkling with distaste.

"Has he been here tonight?"

"No, not yet."

"Do you expect him."

"Yes," she said, sadly.

"I'd like to wait for him."

"Do you want to kill him?"

"Would you like me to?"

Putting her elbows on her desk and leaning forward, Miss Ting said, eagerly, "I will pay you to."

"Why don't you have Lee do it?"

"Oh, he could."

"It would be my pleasure," Lee agreed.

"But we would not be able to afford the trouble it would bring," Miss Ting said.

"With the Barbary Coast Tong?"

"Yes."

"Wait a minute," Tracker said, understanding. "Did the Tong back you in this place?"

"Yes."

"I thought their businesses were only on the Coast."

"Not all," she said. "They own a piece of a few businesses here in Chinatown. Some of us couldn't have gotten started without them."

Tracker noticed that her accent came and went with the size of her speech patterns. If she spoke more than one sentence, it went.

"And now you'd like to get rid of them."

"I don't mind giving them a percentage," she said. "I just wish someone other than Mannion would come to collect it. He always takes one of my girls upstairs, and she's not much good after he gets finished with her."

"He's that rough on them?"

"He never has sex with them, he just beats them up."

"I see."

"Will you kill him? If you kill him, we won't be blamed."

"No, I will."

"You are a big man," she said. "You can take care of yourself. You obviously are not afraid of the Tong or you would not be seeking Mannion."

The accent was back, even though the statement had been more than one sentence long. When she said Mannion's name, she pronounced the two syllables very distinctly, "Man-yon." She was trying to use the accent on him the way Helen Chow had used her body.

"What makes you think I'm an enemy of the Tong?" he asked. "Why couldn't I be a friend of Mannion's?"

For a moment he saw the fear in her eyes and then she overcame it and said, "That monster doesn't have any friends."

"Your accent keeps slipping."

"Yeah, well—" she said, smiling crookedly.

"I'll wait around awhile and see if he shows up. If he doesn't, I'll have a proposal for you before I leave."

"You can wait outside," she said.

"All that crystal will blind me," he said. "Besides, Mannion would recognize me."

"Very well, then you can wait upstairs with one of the girls."

"On the house?"

"Will you kill Mannion?" The woman had a one-track mind.

"I can't promise anything, but it might very well come to that. Let's just say that I wouldn't be all that unhappy if it turned out that I had to."

"And I won't have to pay you?"

"No."

"Lee, take Mr...."

"Tracker, just Tracker."

She nodded and said, "Take Tracker outside and give him his choice of any girl he wants. Make sure you inform him if Mannion shows up. If he does not by the time Tracker leaves, bring him back here."

"As you wish," Lee said with a short bow. "This way, please?"

"Enjoy your wait, Tracker," Miss Ting said.

"I'll sure try."

108

Lu Hom was having very little luck finding out who killed his sister, and it frustrated him. His business had always been to inflict pain on people, use force to collect what was owed. In the past the debt had always been somebody else's. Now, however, the debt was due him and he was at a loss because his specialty was collecting, only he had no one to collect from—yet.

As much as he hated to do it, he knew that he had to pin his hopes on Tracker. Let the big man find out who had killed Anna, and then Lu Hom would be able to collect the debt owed him.

His frustration brought him back to the opium den he was using as his base. He found the message from Tracker waiting for him.

"Miss Ting's?"

"That is what the gentleman said," the elderly doorman replied.

"What is he doing at Miss Ting's?"

"What would one normally do at Miss Ting's?" the older man asked wisely.

"I do not believe it," Lu Hom said. He felt annoyed because he wasn't sure whether he believed it or not. What was Tracker doing at Miss Ting's if not the obvious?

Lu Hom decided to go and find out.

The choice was not an easy one to make. All of Miss Ting's girls were desirable, each in her own way. He finally narrowed the choice down to five.

Tina was Chinese, and reminded him very much of Anna. She had the same long, black hair that was the Chinese woman's trademark. Her body was not quite as full as Anna's had been, but was more bountiful than Helen Chow's, though not as exquisitely formed.

Cathy Lee was a blonde, and very full-bodied, but he decided against her because he would be thinking about another blonde while with her, and that wouldn't do much for his performance.

Rachel was a redhead, but he finally decided against her for the same reason he decided against Cathy Lee. (His feelings for Shana and Deirdre were certainly not making it easy for him to be with other women. He was going to have to examine that when he had the time.)

Molly had long, fine brown hair, freckles, and a willowy body. Her eyes were too close together and her mouth was too wide, but the combination was devastating.

The fifth girl was the only black in Miss Ting's house. She had large breasts and a full, firm ass, full lips—and she was almost six feet tall. Her name was Danielle, and she claimed to be half Cajun.

"You," he said, finally, and then turned to Molly and said, "and you."

The other girls looked at him expectantly, but he smiled and said, "I'm sorry, girls, but I'm not as young as I used to be."

[21]

The next two hours were the most incredible of Tracker's life. The two women were experienced, inventive, uninhibited and very, very eager. The first three qualities were necessary for their profession, but Tracker felt that the latter, the eagerness, was sincere.

When they undressed him they seemed honestly impressed by his physical attributes, and he was certainly pleased with theirs.

Before undressing him they first undressed for him. Molly pulled her dress over her in no-nonsense fashion, revealing her streamlined body. Her breasts were small, but her brown nipples were wide and incredibly long. Her butt was almost boyish, but firm, and her belly was flat. But there was nothing boyish about the moist pink slit between her legs.

Danielle undressed more slowly for him, unveiling herself little by little. Her breasts were very large and full, and her nipples were dark chocolate brown against her light brown skin. Her belly was convex, unlike Molly's, but then Danielle was a big, big lady. Her thighs were meaty and her ass was full with firm, round cheeks.

Next, they undressed him, first removing his shirt and then—after he removed his gunbelt and hung it within easy reach—they took off his pants. Their breath caught when they saw his massive erection, and they immediately went to work on it. They took turns, first Molly taking it into her mouth while Danielle licked his balls, and then switching. At one point they forced him down onto his back on the bed—the sheets *were* clean—and began to lick the length of his shaft, one on each side. Their tongues flicked out and neither girl seemed to mind the contact they were making with each other while they worked on him. As they reached the

111

swollen head their lips met in a juicy kiss with the head of his cock between them.

"Jesus," Tracker said, reaching for one or the other of the girls.

"Relax, baby," Molly said, pushing his hands away. "We're gonna take good care of you."

"That's right," Danielle said, enthusiastically. "This is party time for us, instead of having some fat and sweaty shopkeeper who's hiding from his wife."

The girls exchanged looks and seemed to have agreed without words on what their next move would be. Molly opened her mouth wide and took as much of Tracker's cock into it as she could while fondling his balls. Danielle moved up, sat on Tracker's chest and asked, "Have you ever tasted a black woman before?"

"Never," Tracker said, staring at her crotch which was inches from his mouth.

"Would you like to?" she asked, sliding up to bring her fragrant bush closer to him.

"Very much."

She slid up again and her pubic hair was tickling his nose. He put his tongue out and licked her moist pussy lips up and down.

"How do you like it?"

"I need a bigger taste." As he said that he reached behind her to grasp the full cheeks of her ass and pulled her crotch tight against his face so that she was almost sitting on his face. He thrust his tongue out and it plunged deeply into the sweet depths of her.

"Oh yeah," she breathed as he darted his tongue in and out. At the same time he began to move his hips as Molly increased the tempo of her sucking. His cock was sliding in and out of the white girl's mouth while his tongue slid in and out of the black girl's cunt. When his thighs began to tremble in anticipation of his climax he found Danielle's swollen clit and began to lash it with his tongue. Quickly he brought her to the brink of completion and, when he began to shoot a geyser into Molly's mouth, he clamped down on Danielle with his lips and began to suck furiously, bringing her off at the same time. She bounced up and down on his face, wetting his cheeks as well as his mouth, while Molly reached beneath him to cup his buttocks as she sucked him dry.

After that the girls exchanged positions, and Molly was considerably lighter on his chest and face. Danielle began to lick his cock, trying to bring it back to fullness again, while he held Molly by the ass and eagerly tongued her pussy while she held him by the ears, trying to drown him in her wetness. Danielle moaned appreciatively as he swelled in her mouth, and things followed a familiar pattern: at the same time he brought Molly off, he exploded into the black girl's mouth.

"Oh, Jesus, you girls have sucked me dry," he said as they lay one on each side of him.

"You're not through, are you?" Molly asked, pouting.

"I think it's dead," he said, looking down to where his penis lay in Danielle's hand.

The two girls smiled lasciviously and Molly said, "We have a sure-fire way to bring it back to life."

"You think so?"

"We know so," Danielle said.

"Well," Tracker said with great interest, "give it your best try. Where do I have to be?"

"Just move over, honey," Molly said, "and watch."

Tracker moved over to give them room on the large bed and then watched with mounting interest as the girls embraced.

First they kissed, openmouthed with a lot of tongue action, and they seemed to genuinely enjoy it. While they were kissing their hands were also working. Danielle reached between Molly's legs and began to use her fingers on the white girl while Molly caressed Danielle's big breasts, tweaking the nipples between her fingers. The sight of the two girls kissing and handling each other was already bringing Tracker back to life. It was the most erotic, sexual thing that the big man had ever seen.

He watched in fascination as Molly gradually assumed a dominant position on top of the black girl, sucking and biting her nipples while inserting a couple of fingers into her vagina. Danielle began to moan appreciatively as Molly kissed and licked her down her body until at last her face was nestled between the bigger woman's legs. Tracker leaned closer so that he could see Molly's tongue darting in and out of Danielle's cunt. The black girl was thrashing about on the bed in

113

ecstasy, whipping her head from side to side while Molly licked her slit up and down, pausing at her clit.

"Oh, honey," Danielle gasped, "bring it up here, baby."

Tracker watched as Molly reversed her position. Her face was still buried in Danielle's crotch, but now her own moist pussy was hovering over the other girl's face. Danielle reached out for Molly's ass and pulled her down so that her face was buried and her tongue was busily returning the favor.

Tracker's cock was huge and pulsating by the time both girls achieved a shattering climax, and both looked at him breathlessly and said, "See?"

"I see."

Molly reached out and lovingly ran her hand over Tracker's raging erection. "Now it's time for us to use that giant tool of yours."

"Fine with me. Who's first?"

"Let's do it this way," Danielle suggested, and went on to explain.

What they did was alternate taking Tracker's cock deep into their cunts as he pumped ten times into one girl and ten times into the other, and then switched again, with a friendly bet on which girl he would finally shoot his load into.

Both girls lay down side by side. Tracker entered Molly first and her eyes widened as the length of him easily slid into her well-oiled chasm. She wrapped her legs around his waist and he proceeded to ride her hard while she drummed her heels on his buttocks. After the tenth stroke he slid out of her and moved over to Danielle. The black girl eagerly opened her meaty thighs to him and he rammed her, bringing a gasp to her throat. She wrapped her considerably more powerful legs around him and he rode her the same way he had ridden Molly, which was part of the bargain. Finally, he exploded deep inside Danielle's hot, cavernous channel as Molly watched with envy.

"Oh, God, Molly," Danielle cried out, "it's incredible."

Molly, not wanting to be totally left out, slithered down so that her head was between them at the juncture where they were joined. She used her tongue to

114

avidly lick both of them while Tracker's huge rod pulsed and pumped, emptying inside Danielle.

At that moment the door slammed open and Lu Hom exploded into the room.

[22]

After Tracker had gotten the two girls dressed and out of the room, he turned to face Lu Hom, who had been staring at him murderously since entering. The Chinaman was angry, but Tracker noticed that this hadn't kept him from watching from the corner of his eyes while the two girls dressed. It was nice to know that the man was human, after all.

Tracker waited until he had pulled on his pants before speaking to Lu Hom.

"What the hell is wrong with you?"

"Is this how you look for the murderer of my sister?" Lu Hom demanded.

"I'm working on it, Lu."

"Why were you here fornicating with those two whores, then?"

"Because it was a way to kill time," Tracker said, reaching for his shirt. "In fact, it was a damned good way to do it."

"I do not understand."

"Well, if you'd ask nicely for an explanation instead of barging in the way you did, I'd help you understand."

Lu Hom blinked twice and then said, "Very well. I am asking for an explanation."

Tracker gave him one. He told him how he was waiting for Mannion to show up at the whorehouse, but did not want to wait downstairs for fear the big man would see him.

"And if he does not show up tonight, will you then come here every night and fornicate?"

Tracker, convinced that Lu Hom did not have a sense of humor, refrained from saying that he thought that might not have been such a bad idea.

"No, if he doesn't show up here tonight—and I suspect he won't, maybe even because you scared him off—I have another plan."

"Which is what?"

"Why don't we go downstairs so I can explain it to you and Miss Ting at the same time."

"You want to do what?" Miss Ting asked.

"Put a girl here in your establishment to watch for Mannion. When he comes, she'll handle him."

"She will, eh?" Miss Ting asked, looking dubious. "Is this girl a whore?"

"Uh, no, she's a detective—"

"A detective!"

"—But I can tell you she's got a very definite feel for this business. You might even call it a knack."

Miss Ting still looked doubtful, but she said, "All right, I agree. When will you bring her for me to look at?"

"You want her to apply for the job?"

"I look at every girl that works in my place," Miss Ting said, "and I look very closely. What does this girl look like?"

"She's Chinese."

"That'll be fresh."

"I'll bring her by tomorrow afternoon—I mean, later this afternoon," he said, realizing that it was now well into the next day.

"I'll be waiting."

"She'll be one of your girls by tomorrow night. We should be okay as long as Mannion doesn't come by early this morning for an eye-opener."

"I'm not open that early," the madam said, "even for the Barbary Coast Tong."

"I like a place that sticks to its policies," Tracker said. "We'll see you this afternoon."

Tracker and Lu Hom followed Lee out, pausing only so Tracker could say good-bye and thanks to Molly and Danielle.

"You come back sometime, Tracker," Molly said.

"We didn't show you all our tricks," Danielle added.

"I'll be back," he promised.

Outside Lu Hom said, "I do not know if this plan of yours will work."

"Hell, I don't know if it will, either. That's what we're going to find out."

Lu Hom asked, "What will you do now?"

"I've got to convince a little lady to play whore."

"Will that be a problem?"

"I don't know," Tracker replied honestly. "She's got the talent, I just don't know if she's got the inclination."

[23]

"You asked me that question once before," Helen Chow said, in the morning.

"This time I'm serious."

She frowned, studying him, and then said, "By God, you are serious, aren't you?"

"Yes. Miss Ting is waiting to...inspect you."

"Like a horse?"

"She inspects all the girls who work in her place."

"Do you think I'll pass?"

He grinned and said, "Easily."

"And what am I supposed to do in this whorehouse?"

"Wait for a man called Mannion to come in. When he does, get his attention. Make him want to go upstairs with you, and then keep him there until I get there. Miss Ting will send word to me."

"How long will I have to...keep him occupied?"

"Not long, but I've got to tell you one thing."

"What's that?"

"He likes to beat women up."

"That's wonderful."

"You've got to make him want to take you to bed, not just beat you up."

"And if I can't?"

"Sweetheart, if you can't, nobody can."

"Miss Ting, this is Helen."

Tracker watched the madam's face while she studied Helen Chow, and he could tell that she was impressed.

"Have you ever work as a whore before, my dear?" Miss Ting asked, using her accent.

"No, but I've used sex to get what I want. Does that count?"

"It does, indeed."

119

"And could we drop the accent? I mean, I use it too, at times, but it seems out of place between us."

Miss Ting looked at Tracker and said, "She'll do. Helen, you might try using the accent with our customers. They like it."

"There's only one customer I'm going to concern myself with," Helen said. "When he walks in, that's when I start to work. Not before."

"As you wish," Miss Ting said, "but I would really like to see you in action. If you do well, I might offer you a job at a good wage."

"No, thanks. I'll keep the one I've got."

"I'll check in from time to time," Tracker said to both women, "but as soon as Mannion shows up, send me word at Farrell House. They'll know where I am at all times."

"All right." Miss Ting said to her man, Lee, "See that she has the proper clothes." To Helen: "At least you'll have to dress the part. You have an exquisite body."

"Thank you." Helen Chow had never received such a compliment from another woman.

Tracker put his hand on her arm and drew her aside.

"Let's get serious for just a minute."

"Sure."

"If it begins to look like you can't handle him, then get away from him. I don't expect you to get killed keeping him here for me."

"I'll keep him here," she said with confidence, "but this is going to cost you, Tracker...dearly."

The look in her eyes made no secret of how she intended to collect.

[24]

It didn't take long.

Mannion came to Miss Ting's that evening, looking for his favorite girl: Tina.

"He put me in the hospital once," Tina told Helen, "and broke my arm once. The other times he simply battered me senseless. It is the only way he can justify his manhood."

"How can I get him to choose me?"

"Well, number one is I'll have to be missing. Secondly, don't show him any fear. If I begged him not to choose me, he would probably take someone else, but I would never give the pig the satisfaction."

So when Mannion showed up at the front door of Miss Ting's, the first things Lee did before allowing him to enter was to tell Tina to hide and alert Helen.

Mannion entered the large room and looked around. Everyone knew he was looking for Tina.

When Miss Ting appeared he put the question to her. "Where is she?"

"She's gone. After the last time she was afraid you'd come back again, so she left."

Miss Ting knew that Danielle would give her hell for telling him that, but it was in a good cause.

Mannion said, "Who can I choose, then?"

"Molly?"

"Too skinny."

"Rachel?"

"No," he said, looking around. When his eyes fell on Helen she stared back at him boldly, with a challenge in her eyes.

"Who's the Chink?"

"A new girl. Her name is Helen."

He stared at Helen, and she returned his stare unwaveringly.

"I'll take her."

Miss Ting released the breath she was holding and said, "Very well. I'll tell her."

"*I'll* tell her," he said. He strode over to where Helen was seated and grabbed her by the arm. The man's strength was incredible. "Come with me, Chink."

Miss Ting watched as Mannion dragged Helen upstairs, then looked at Lee and nodded. It was Lee who would go to Farrell House looking for Tracker.

Tracker was at the hotel, having returned from seeing John Cooper, who had given him some interesting information.

Lee presented himself to Deirdre, who had been alerted to wait for his appearance.

When Tracker appeared Lee said, "He is there."

"Then let's go."

Lee used his key to open the front door of Miss Ting's, and when they entered, Tracker could hear the shouts coming from upstairs. As he entered the large waiting room he could see Miss Ting and the others, frozen in their places, all heads turned toward the upstairs.

"Is that him?" Tracker asked.

Miss Ting turned to face him and said, "You better get up there. I think he's killing her."

At that moment there was a scream and it galvanized Tracker into action. He ran up the stairs and located the room where all the shouting was coming from. The door was locked, but one kick was all Tracker needed to snap it open.

Mannion turned and the look on his face was one of excitement, sexual excitement, which he could only get from beating women. When he saw Tracker the look faded from his face and was replaced by one of anger and rage. He was stark naked, and his penis and testicles were huge.

Helen Chow was on the floor, her face a mass of bruises and blood. One arm was twisted beneath her at an unnatural angle, but she was alive.

"You!" Mannion shouted.

"Me," Tracker said. "You want to give me a try, Mannion, or is it only women that you can beat up yourself. When it's a man you have others do it, right?"

"Yah!" Mannion cried out and charged Tracker.

The man's strength was great, Tracker knew that from what he had done to Will Sullivan, but Will had always been a plodder in the ring. He did not have Tracker's speed, nor Tracker's brain.

Tracker sidestepped Mannion's charge and stuck his foot out, tripping the man. As Mannion went down Tracker followed his progress and launched a kick at the man's head. His boot made contact and he heard Mannion grunt, but he did not lose consciousness.

Mannion's hand clawed frantically for his gun and Tracker decided not to play games with him. He was far too dangerous.

He drew his own gun and brought it down with bone-jarring force on Mannion's gunhand. He could feel the bones shatter and the other man let out an anguished scream. He rolled over on the floor, cradling his injured hand against his chest, whimpering.

"It's always the cruel ones," Tracker said, "the ones who like to inflict pain, who can't take it."

He removed Mannion's gun from his holster, then turned his attention to Helen. Her lovely face was a mess and her arm was broken. He didn't know what other injuries she might have had.

"Helen, dammit, I told you to stay out of his way."

She grinned through her split lips and said, "I had him going for a while."

"Yeah."

Miss Ting and Lee entered the room then and Tracker said, "Get her to a doctor."

Miss Ting motioned to Lee, who went to help Helen to her feet and take her from the room. Miss Ting herself walked over to where Mannion lay, holding his injured hand, and she kicked him in the crotch. His eyes bulged and he didn't know whether to hold his hand or his testicles.

"Leave enough of him to talk, Miss Ting," Tracker said.

"That's all I wanted to do," she said to Tracker. "He's all yours, now."

She left the room and Tracker went and leaned over Mannion.

"All right, Mannion, I'm going to ask you a few questions and you're going to answer. If you don't," Tracker said, pushing the barrel of his gun against the man's aching balls, "I'm going to shoot them off."

"Jesus," Mannion moaned, "you can't—"

Tracker prodded him with the gun, causing him to jump, and said, "Want to bet?"

"Jesus—" Mannion said between clenched teeth.

Tracker cocked his gun and said, "First question. Who killed Anna Ching?"

Tracker had to prod him one more time before he blurted, "I did, I did."

"And where is Melody Tinsdale?"

"I don't know." Poke. "I swear, I don't know!"

"What about a diamond?"

"I don't know anything about no diamond."

Tracker believed him. Mannion didn't know about Melody and the Tinsdale diamond, but did that mean that the Tong leader didn't know, either?

"One more question, Mannion. Where do I find the head of the Barbary Coast Tong?"

"He'll have me killed—"

"I'll kill you now, dammit! Where?"

Mannion told him and Tracker believed him—but he couldn't believe it. California Street was the last place he expected to find the Tong leader.

"That's it, Mannion," Tracker said. "I've got everything I need from you."

Mannion looked into Tracker's eyes and knew that he was a dead man.

"Hold it right there, Tracker," a voice said from the doorway. Tracker recognized the voice.

"Colby."

"That's right," Inspector Colby said.

"You here officially?"

"No. I finally found out that Mannion liked to come here and thought I'd keep watch until he showed up."

Tracker still hadn't turned around to look at the man.

"How'd you find out about him?"

"I've known for some time that Mannion worked for

the Tong, but he was never the one I wanted—until now. He killed Anna, didn't he?"

"Yes."

"Get out of the way."

"You holding a gun on me, Colby?"

"Yes."

"Put it up."

"Not until you move out of the way."

"You want to kill him?"

"You bet I do."

"If you don't put up your gun, I'll pull the trigger on mine. You won't get your chance."

Silence prevailed while Colby thought, and Mannion was too frightened to speak.

"What's it going to be, Colby?"

Tracker heard a thud, and then what sounded like a body hitting the floor.

"Tracker," another voice said.

"That you, Lu Hom?"

"Yes. The Inspector is no longer holding a gun on you."

Tracker stood up, backed away from Mannion and then turned his head. He saw Lu Hom standing in the doorway, straddling the still form of Colby.

"You kill him?"

"No. Is that the man who killed my sister?"

"Yes."

"He is mine."

"Yes," Tracker said. He agreed that Lu Hom had prior claim to Mannion because Anna was his sister. Putting up his gun, Tracker stepped over Colby's body and said, "He's all yours, Lu. Bring the Inspector down with you when you're finished."

Tracker went down the stairs to the waiting room where Miss Ting and the others had made Helen comfortable while they waited for a doctor.

"Helen...."

She looked up at Tracker from the cushioned couch she was lying on.

"Did you get what you wanted?" she asked. One eye had closed and the bruises on her face had swelled even more.

"Some, not all. I found out who killed Anna Ching, but he didn't know anything about Melody Tinsdale."

"Why would he?" Miss Ting asked.

"Her father hired me to find her. He thought that maybe the Barbary Coast Tong had taken her to sell—"

"That's nonsense."

Tracker frowned and looked up at Miss Ting.

"You've got her, don't you?" he asked.

"I don't have her," Miss Ting said, "but she's here."

"I should have known."

"Why?"

"I just found out today that you've got a diamond on the market. It's her diamond, isn't it?"

"Yes. She wanted me to sell it to get her enough money to get out of San Francisco and get away from her father."

"Where is she?"

Miss Ting looked at Lee, who left the room, presumably to return with Melody Tinsdale.

John Cooper had sent for Tracker earlier that day to tell him that the diamond had finally shown up on the market, and that it was Miss Ting who was trying to sell. He'd planned to ask the madam about it, but it hadn't occurred to him that she might have Melody in her whorehouse.

"Uh, she's not...working here, is she?"

Miss Ting sighed and said, "Would that she would. She's a lovely girl—well, you can see for yourself."

Melody Tinsdale had changed substantially since the tintype her father had given Tracker. Her body had filled out considerably, her hair was the color of wheat and she looked older than he knew she was.

"We've been keeping her here under the name Cathy Lee," Miss Ting said.

Melody/Cathy Lee was one of the girls Tracker had almost chosen the day before.

"Melody."

"You were hired by my father?"

"Yes."

"I'll pay you not to tell him you found me."

"We'll talk later, okay? Where the hell's that doctor?"

126

At that moment Lee brought a man with a black bag into the room and, as he did, Lu Hom came down the stairs carrying Inspector Colby as if he weighed next to nothing.

"I understood I only had one patient."

"He's just got a bump on the head," Tracker said, as Lu dumped the unconscious Inspector into a chair.

"You've got two patients," Miss Ting said. "There's one upstairs."

"No," Lu Hom said, "there is not. You have one patient."

The doctor looked at Helen and decided to treat the patient he saw and not worry about anything else.

Miss Ting looked at Lu Hom, then at Tracker.

"Is he going to want to be paid?" she asked. "My deal was with you."

"He's had his payment already, Miss Ting." The woman frowned at him and he clarified it by adding, "Revenge."

[25]

They woke Colby up and Tracker convinced him to calm down and accompany him back to Farrell House. Lu Hom was already gone at that point so that the lawman wouldn't be tempted to try to arrest him.

"Why should I come back to your hotel with you," Colby demanded, touching the back of his neck, "and who hit me?"

"I told you. One of the girls saw you holding a gun on me and let you have it. As to why you should come back with me, I would think you'd want to be in on the closing down of the Barbary Coast Tong."

"What?"

"After all, Mannion may have killed Anna Ching, but he would have been ordered to by the Tong leader."

"And you know who he is?"

"No, but I know where to find him."

"All right, then. I'll come back with you."

"You might want to let Preston in on this—"

"The hell with him!" Colby said with disgust.

"All right. Wait for me by the door, I've got some business to take care of here."

Tracker also instructed Melody that she was still playing Cathy Lee as far as Inspector Colby was concerned. When she asked why, he once again told her that they would talk later.

When he showed up at the front door with Melody/Cathy Lee in tow, Colby asked, "Where is she going?"

"With me."

"What for?"

"My reward."

"What about that Chinese girl who was beaten up?"

"She was taken to the hospital. She'll be all right."

Tracker wanted to keep Helen Chow's identity from

Colby, as well. In fact, he wanted to keep the lawman in the dark about as much as he could for as long as he could.

"Let's get back to the hotel," he said, "and we can make plans."

Colby looked at Cathy Lee and said, "I hope we're thinking about the same kind of plans."

When Tracker entered the lobby of Farrell House Duke noticed the cop with Tracker, and Deirdre noticed the blonde.

"What's he doing here?" Duke said aloud.

"For that matter, what's she doing here?" Deirdre asked.

"I guess we'll find out," he murmered as Tracker approached the desk.

"Duke, take Inspector Colby into the dining room and get him a drink. He's got a bit of a pain in the neck."

Duke frowned, wondering what the joke was, but said, "Sure, but—"

"I'll be down in a moment to talk with him, and I'd like you to sit in."

"All right, Tracker."

As Duke took the young cop's arm and led him toward the dining room Deirdre said, "And what about me? You want me to take your new girlfriend into the bar and get her a drink?"

"I want you to give her a room—"

"How many girls do you want to have in this hotel?"

"Dee, this is important."

Deirdre scolded herself mentally, because it obviously was important to him.

"All right. Here," she said, grabbing a key. "I'll register her. What name?"

"Cathy Lee."

"That's it?"

"It's two names, isn't it? It'll do."

"All right."

"Thanks, Dee."

Tracker palmed the key and went and took Melody's arm.

"Come on. I got you a room where we can talk."

129

Once they were in the room Tracker turned the girl around to face him and stared right at her face.

"You've got a hell of a lot of paint on your face."

Melody smiled and looked her age for the first time since he'd seen her.

"Miss Ting said it would change the way my face looked."

"She was right. Why don't you get cleaned up and I'll see about getting you some clothes. You could catch cold in that dress."

The front of the dress plunged, which had gotten her a lot of attention during the trip from Miss Ting's to the hotel.

"I'd appreciate it."

"Melody, tell me something."

"What?"

"Why Miss Ting's?"

"Oh, I met one of the girls—Molly—and told her that I had left home with no money. All I had was the diamond my father had given me."

"Which Miss Ting still has."

"I want her to sell it."

"Yes," Tracker said, seeing his fee going south.

"My father just wants to run me the way he runs his politicians, and I can't live like that. The money from the diamond will help me get away. Anyway, Molly brought me to Miss Ting's and the madam agreed to let me stay there until she sold the diamond."

"Out of the goodness of her heart, right?"

"And half what she got for the diamond," Melody admitted, "but it's worth it to me."

"We're going to get that rock back from Miss Ting, Melody—"

"But I don't want to."

"I'll sell it for you and you won't have to split the money with anyone."

"Really?"

"Yes."

"Oh, thank you, Tracker."

She threw her arms around his neck, flattened her plump breasts against his chest and kissed him, pushing her tongue between his lips.

"You're not going to tell my father where I am, are

130

you?" she asked. Her eyes were very wide and innocent, and her tongue was tracing the line of his mouth.

"We'll figure that out, too," he told her, unwinding her arms from his neck.

"Together?"

"Yes," he said, "together."

"Hurry back."

Tracker's job was finished. Melody Tinsdale was safe, and he knew where the stone was and could get it anytime he wanted. Why then was he on his way down to the dining room to make plans with Colby to storm the headquarters of the Barbary Coast Tong? For Helen Chow? For Colby, because Tracker knew what it felt like to lose Anna Ching? What about Lu Hom?

Or maybe it had just been too long since he'd busted up a tong.

[26]

As Tracker reached the lobby he saw Lu Hom come through the front door.

"Glad you could make it," Tracker said.

"Where is Colby?"

"In the dining room. Are we going to have a problem between the two of you?"

"No."

"It looks like we're going to have to bring down another tong, eh, Lu?"

"It was for my sister last time, and it is for her, again." Lu Hom pinned a stare on Tracker and said, "It will not happen again."

Tracker did not doubt Lu Hom's words.

"Let's go inside before Colby gets too drunk to help us."

"Why do we need him?"

"The answer to that is easy," Tracker said. "He's a cop and he gives us some official status. That can't hurt us."

Lu Hom didn't comment, he simply followed Tracker into the dining room.

"What's he doing here?" Colby demanded when he saw Lu Hom.

"He's got a right," Tracker said. "Anna was his sister."

Colby stared at Lu Hom, who glared back, and when neither man spoke again Tracker said, "Let's get started," and he and the Chinaman sat down.

It didn't take very long for them to formulate a plan. Actually, Tracker laid the whole thing out for them and then waited for their reactions.

"Am I in on this?" Duke asked.

"In a small way," Tracker said. "You won't be coming along, but I want your opinion."

"I think you're crazy."

"Why?"

"You don't know how many men this tong has got in this place on California Street."

"We'll find out," Tracker said. He turned to Lu Hom and Colby and said, "Okay, you fellas are going with me. What do you say?"

"I think it's crazy, too," Colby said, "but I can't think of a better way."

"And you?"

"I will go with you."

"Okay, then. Do we go tonight, or tomorrow?"

"Tonight," Colby said.

Tracker looked at Lu Hom, who said, "Now."

He looked at Duke, who said, "You're all crazy."

"All right, that's it then. You two wait for me in the lobby, I've got to talk to Duke for a minute."

Colby and Lu Hom both rose, staring at each other, and walked away from the table together, keeping three or four feet between them.

"I think you're even crazier to go with those two. They don't like each other."

"Yeah, and I'm expecting a Christmas present from both of them, right?"

"Crazy."

"All right, listen. There's a girl in room 214. She's registered as Cathy Lee, but her name is Melody Tinsdale."

"Tinsdale?"

"Right. Get her some clothes and something to eat and make sure nothing happens to her."

"Until you get back."

"Right."

Tracker started to get up and Duke said, "If you come back."

Tracker paused and said, "Uh, yeah."

"Hey, what's the name of this place on California Street that you and your troops are storming tonight?"

"The last place I would have thought of," Tracker said. "The Crystal Palace."

[27]

Tracker went into the Crystal Palace first, after ascertaining whether or not Colby thought he would be recognized.

"I'm still fairly new in San Francisco and, although I've pretty much made a pest of myself on the Barbary Coast, I think I could get away with it for a while."

"Okay. If someone recognizes you, just see if you can't keep them quiet for a while. We don't want this thing to blow up in our faces. We don't know how many of the people who will be in the Palace are Tong members."

Lu Hom, it was decided, would do one of the things that he did best, stay in the shadows and use them to keep out of sight until he was needed—when all hell broke loose.

As Tracker entered the Crystal Palace he wondered what Crystal Hale's part in all of this would turn out to be. Surely, the Tong couldn't be using the Palace as a headquarters without her knowing it.

He went to the bar where his old friend was tending bar.

"What—"

"Easy, friend. I just want a drink. I don't have to knock you on your ass to get that, do I?"

"What'll you have?"

"A beer."

The man brought him a beer and then faded toward the far end of the bar.

Tracker stayed at the bar, examining the room and nursing his beer until Colby walked in. He watched the crowd to see if he could spot any positive reaction to the lawman's appearance, but as far as he could see, the young Inspector had gone unnoticed.

Colby went to the bar, leaving plenty of room between himself and Tracker, and ordered a beer. Now that his backup was there, it was time for Tracker to go into action.

He waved the bartender over and asked, "Where's Crystal tonight?"

"Upstairs."

"Get her."

"What?"

"I said, get her."

"She's, uh, busy right now. She won't take kindly to be interrupted."

"She with her little friend?"

"I don't—"

"Look, friend, I'm only going to tell you this one more time—get her!"

"Okay, all right," the man said, looking as if he were afraid that Tracker would drag him across the bar. "I'll get her."

"I'll wait."

Tracker finished his beer while he was waiting, keeping his eyes on the crowds around the gambling tables. He was very careful not to look over at Colby.

Presently the bartender came scurrying down the steps and, avoiding Tracker's eyes, resumed his position behind the bar.

"Well?" Tracker asked.

"She's coming—but she ain't happy."

"That's tough."

Tracker watched carefully while Crystal came down the steps slowly and he could see that she wasn't happy. The smile on her face was strained and he wondered if she sensed that he had not come back simply to share her bed, and her little friend.

"Tracker. You scared my bartender half to death. Why didn't you just come up—"

"I have a feeling it's going to be safer down here, Crystal, where it's crowded."

"Are you afraid of me?" she asked, contriving to sound playful.

"No, but maybe you should be afraid of me," he said. "Mannion's dead."

There was a split second where she didn't seem to

know how she should react. Then she looked surprised and asked, "Did you kill him?"

"No, but I was there. I spoke to him before he died."

"Really?"

"Yeah. He told me where to find the leader of the Barbary Coast Tong."

"Is that so? Where?"

"Here."

She paused and then asked, "At the Palace? My place?"

"Don't play cute with me, Crystal. If you want to come out of this in one piece, tell me where he is. I'm not here to play games."

She only took a few seconds to make her decision and then she said, "Downstairs."

"How many men does he have with him?"

"I don't know," she said, sounding weary. "He doesn't keep bodyguards around. He never expected to be found."

That arrogance would, Tracker hoped, work against the leader, and to Tracker's advantage.

"Are any of these people his men?"

"Tracker, they could all be and I wouldn't know it. The only one I ever knew was Mannion."

Tracker looked around the place again. There were no Chinese present, although he knew that the Tong used them. What he didn't know was if they were used as messenger boys—or hatchet men.

"All right, show me how to get down there."

"Tracker, I didn't have any choice. I had to let him—"

"Save it for later, Crystal. Just show me how to get down to where he is."

She nodded and said, "Follow me."

Tracker made a concerted effort not to check and see if Colby was following his progress.

Crystal led him past the stairway and through a curtained doorway.

"There's a door here that leads downstairs. I-I've never been down there."

"All right. Stay up here and out of the way. I'm going down."

"Be careful."

Sure, he thought, of what's down there . . . and of you.

136

As he descended the steps he hoped that Colby would be smart enough to keep his eyes on Crystal Hale.

The stairwell was dark, but he could see a thin line of light at the foot of the stairway, light showing from beneath a door. When he reached the door he drew his gun and tried the knob. As a testament to the Tong leader's arrogance, the door was unlocked.

Tracker decided to open it slowly instead of bursting into the room. As he did so he could hear what sounded like a girl moaning. As he listened further and heard sucking sounds, he decided that she wasn't being tortured. From the sounds she was making, she was engaged in something more intimate and amorous than torture.

"That's it, girl," a man's voice said, "you're getting the hang of it. You'll be ready to send out soon, and I'll have to break in somebody new."

"Oh, master," the girl said, "if I please you won't you keep me here with you?"

"I'm sorry, my dear, but you are already bought and paid for," the man said, and Tracker knew he was in the right place.

He opened the door wide, stepped into the room and saw that the man was facing the door, but was looking down at the bobbing head of the girl on her knees before him. She was moaning and making sucking noises again, and Tracker felt that they were the kind of sounds that whores made when they were trying to convince a man that they were enjoying themselves.

He stepped further into the room and quietly closed the door behind him. Holding his gun up at his shoulder but pointed at the ceiling he waited for a lull in the noises the girl was making. Then he cocked his gun.

"Hello," he said aloud.

The man's head jerked up and he stared wide-eyed at Tracker. He was naked, and he wasn't built for it. His belly was round and sloppy, and his hair was gray and thinning. His hands were cupping the back of the girl's head and the girl was still going on about her business, oblivious to Tracker's presence. Apparently she was very intent on doing a good job. Even from behind she looked young, and he was sure she was one of the products of his white slavery ring, and not a pro.

"Who are you?" the man demanded.

"What are you doing with my sister?" Tracker said.

The man's mouth dropped open and he said, "Y-your sister. What are you talking—"

"What's wrong—" the girl started to say, but the man pushed her away so that she went sprawling.

"I don't know who you are—"

"But I know who you are," Tracker said. "You're the leader of the Barbary Coast Tong, Mannion's boss, right?"

"Mannion," the man said, beginning to panic. "He'll kill you—"

"Mannion's dead."

"Wha—" the man said, looking shocked. "He can't be. I-I need him."

The man looked pitiful standing there naked, his erection—which hadn't been that big to begin with—rapidly shriveling. He was not what Tracker had pictured when he thought of the Tong leader.

Something was wrong.

"I think I get it," Tracker said. "You're a puppet."

"What?"

"You're the front man, and this is the first time you've been threatened. Man, you're falling apart."

"This wasn't supposed to happen," the man said anxiously. "This wasn't ever supposed to happen!"

"But it has, and you're on the hot seat, friend," Tracker said, pointing the gun at the frightened man. The leader was probably a big man with his underlings, because they were afraid of him. This was a whole different story.

"As far as I'm concerned you're the leader," Tracker told him, "and I'm about to put an end to that."

"No, don't shoot!" the man said, falling to his knees and holding his hands out in front of him to ward off the bullets. The girl had crawled into a corner and was watching the whole thing with frightened eyes.

"Then talk to me."

He lowered his hands away from his face and looked at Tracker.

"What do you want to know?"

"You're the puppet," Tracker said, "and I want to know who pulls the strings."

"I can't—"

"Listen, friend, I haven't killed anybody today and if you don't tell me what I want to know, you're just going to make my day."

Tracker sighted down the barrel and the kneeling man began to blubber incoherently. He was facing a situation he had obviously been assured he would never have to face, and he was going to pieces in the face of it.

"Talk to me!"

"Die!" a woman's voice said from the door, and a shot was fired from behind Tracker. A red hole blossomed in the kneeling man's chest, and he fell onto his face.

"Don't turn around, Tracker," Crystal Hale said.

"Going to shoot me in the back?"

"No," she said, "I'm going to offer you a deal. If you don't take it, then I'm going to have to shoot you in the back."

"Go ahead, then," he said, "make your pitch."

"First drop your gun."

Tracker hesitated, then dropped it.

"Kick it."

He obeyed, kicking it away from him.

"If you're counting on your friends helping you, forget it. They're busy upstairs, busting up my place."

"Sorry for the inconvenience."

"That's all it is, really. I've got the money to fix it."

"Glad to hear it."

"You want to hear my offer?"

"Why not? What have I got to lose?"

"Shall I tell you?"

"Just talk."

"That man was an actor," she said, meaning the dead man on the floor. "I set him up as the Tong leader and he played the part okay with the chinks. He even had Mannion convinced."

"Did Mannion know about you?"

"No, he thought that Henry—that was his name—was the leader."

"And all the time it was you."

"Right, and now I need a new front man."

"Why?"

139

"If the rest of the men in the Tong knew that they were working for a woman I think I'd lose them."

"Hire others?"

"That's what I need a man like you for, Tracker. You're strong. You could do what it took both Henry and Mannion to do—and you could have me."

"Well, that's what I call a tempting offer. Can I turn around and take a look at what I'll be getting? It might help my decision."

"Sure, honey. Turn around."

He turned and saw her holding a .32 on him. The way she'd killed the man she called Henry, he had no doubt that she'd shoot him, as well.

"What do you say?"

"That's not a very big gun."

"And you're a very big man." She shrugged and added, "So I'll keep pulling the trigger until it's empty. You know, Tracker, I think maybe I've withdrawn my offer. It's too bad, you really are a beautiful man—but you're also dangerous."

She extended her arm and he tensed, wondering how close he could get to her before she pumped him so full of lead that he'd weigh more dead than he did alive.

There was a shot and Tracker's stomach muscles jumped. He watched in fascination as the top of Crystal's blonde head dissolved into a bloody mess.

Tracker turned and looked over at the naked young girl who had been making all the noise over Henry's manhood when he entered. She was holding his gun in both hands and pointing it at him.

"What's your name?" he asked.

"Shari."

"Shari, that's my gun."

"I-I know."

"Would you like to give it back to me?"

"I-I—"

"Would you like to go home?"

"Yes," she said, jumping on that one.

"Well," he said, taking a careful step toward her, "if you give me my gun, I'll take you home."

She had her choice. She could trust him and give him the gun, or she could assume that he was like the

140

other men she'd been given to since she was taken by the Tong and kill him!

"Come on, Shari," he said softly, "let me take you home."

The girl studied him for what seemed like a few years, then nodded and held the gun out to him.

"Take me home?"

He had just gotten the girl dressed when Colby and Lu Hom appeared at the door and stepped over the bloody corpse of Crystal Hale.

"Was that him?" Colby asked.

"What took you guys so long?"

"There were a lot of them up there," Colby said, "and they all came at me at once. If it wasn't for Lu Hom, I'd be dead meat, right now."

"It works both ways," Lu Hom said.

"Great, you two guys made friends while I was almost shot."

"We are not friends," Lu Hom said.

"Is that him?" Colby asked again, pointing to the dead man. "Was that the head of the Barbary Coast Tong?"

"That's what everybody thought," Tracker told them, "but the real leader is behind you."

Both men whirled quickly, and when they saw no one in the doorway they looked down at the dead Crystal Hale.

"You got it," Tracker said. "She wasn't just the leader. She *was* the Barbary Coast Tong."

[28]

When Tracker got back to Farrell House he knew that there were still a lot of things he should do:

He should check on Helen Chow's condition.

He should check on Melody Tinsdale and make sure she was all right.

He should go to Miss Ting's and get the diamond.

He should get word to Tinsdale that his daughter was safe, but not coming home. He hoped the man would be satisfied with that knowledge.

Preston would be breathing down his neck soon, he knew, even though Colby had let him and Lu Hom leave before sending for the police chief, so he should probably set up an alibi for the night, as well.

He was bone-weary when he entered the lobby of the hotel and very few things could have made him feel otherwise.

Seeing Shana behind the desk was one of those things.

"Shana—"

She looked up at him and the strain of the past few days showed on her lovely face.

"How's Will?"

"He's fine," she said. "He made it."

He closed his eyes and if he were a religious man he would have thanked God.

"Shana, I'm sorry—"

"No," she said, cutting him off. "Will and I talked and he made me see that it wasn't your fault. He's a grown man and he can make his own decisions. This was one of them."

"Yes."

"I-I just need a little time, Tracker, to let it sink in. Okay?"

"Sure."